1

Special thanks to my

Very good friend

Dave Smith.

His assistance is invaluable.

His friendship revered.

Preface

What could be better than spending a pleasant day at the races? When Private Investigator Flats Magull, bumps into a renowned horse trainer friend, he is invited to the upcoming Cheltenham festival as a guest. Being a keen follower of the sport of Kings, Flats readily accepts and introduces his newly adopted daughter Andrea to horse racing. They are enjoying a wonderful day out when it's announced that his friend's prize winning stallion, and big race favourite, has gone missing. He immediately hires Flats to find the horse, but where do you start looking for such a large beast? His search for the horse uncovers a web of lies, deceit, race fixing and horse doping. The investigation takes a sinister turn when a promising young jockey is found hanged and they find a note. But was it really suicide?

Chapter One

It was early March and spring was in the air as Flats began the day in his garden tending to his chickens. Andrea, his recently adopted daughter, was helping whilst Jeeves his trusty collie was running around sniffing everywhere and stopping occasionally to scrutinize a new scent.

'I think we may have had a visit overnight from a fox, judging by the way Jeeves is behaving.'

'How do you know that?' enquired Andrea.

'It's the way he's going back and forth across the ground trying to work out where the scent comes from. I've seen him do it before and previously it cost me my brood.'

'How can a fox get into the chicken house?'

'They dig under the wire, and when they get in they kill all of the birds, not just one. I need to make the pen more secure so I'll pop to the local farmers store later. What are your plans for today?'

'As Isla has the day off, we are going to Taunton for a bit of shopping. Is there anything that you need?'

Flats shook his head, 'No thank you, I'll have a quick cuppa and then go to the South West Farmers shop, or should I say warehouse.'

'Is it really that big a place?' asked Andrea.

'Oh yes, they sell everything imaginable for farm and domesticated animals, they even have many items of clothing.'

'Really? I'll ask Isla if she fancies going there instead of Taunton, that's if you don't mind us tagging along.'

'You know that both of you are always welcome to accompany me at anytime.'

'Thank you, I'll nip indoors and ask her now.'

As Isla had never been to a farmer's store, she was happy to go. 'We can do Taunton another day,' she said.

After a cup of tea, Flats drove them to the Farmer's supply site. It was very busy because right next door was the livestock market and today happened to be auction day. The two young women were amazed by the sheer size of the place.

'Can we have a look round at the animals?' asked Isla.

Flats nodded, 'Go ahead, I need to get some supplies.'

As he was looking around the store, someone called out to him. 'Hey Flats, is that you?'

He turned to see the familiar face of renowned trainer Kenny Race. 'Hello Ken, long time no see, how are things with you?'

'Very good thanks, how's retirement suiting you? Tell me, do you still follow the horses?'

'It's wonderful not having to go to work and being able to please myself. I've been taking some private detective work which has kept me occupied, but in answer to your second question, yes of course. I've got a TV now, so I can watch races broadcast live on it.'

'How would you like to come to the upcoming Cheltenham festival ...... as my guest of course?' offered Ken.

'I would love to, thank you. Does the invitation extend to a guest of my own?' he asked cheekily.

'It can if I give you a couple of extra passes. Give me a couple of minutes and I'll go and get you a few from my pick-up. I won't be long.'

Ken walked away and disappeared out of the building. Flats continued with his shopping, 'now let me see,' he said out loud as he checked his list. 'Chicken feed, check, dog biscuits and treats, check.' Jeeves barked, 'You are too clever by half, I was talking to myself boy. Now I need some heavy duty chicken wire, a few posts and some galvanized staples.'

Andrea and Isla had entered the building. 'Blimey, this place is huge,' said Andrea as they met up with Flats.

'We should check out the clothing section,' said Isla.

Ken returned and handed Flats an envelope. 'There you go; I've put four passes in there ….. And who are these two lovely young ladies?'

Flats put his arm around one of them. 'This is my adop ….. Sorry, daughter Andrea and my lodger Isla who also happens to be a DS at Yeovil station.'

'I never knew that you had a daughter, I'm very pleased to meet you both. Now if you'll excuse me, I must get on. See you in a couple of weeks Flats, and then we can have a proper catch up.'

'I'll look forward to it,' he replied.

'He seemed very friendly, who was he?' asked Andrea.

'That was Kenny Race, a much respected horse trainer, and an extremely successful one at that. He has just given me some passes to the Cheltenham festival which is in a couple of week's time. I thought perhaps you might like to come with me.'

'Does that invitation extend to me?' begged Isla.

'If you like, I have a couple of spare passes; you'll be welcome to join us.'

'Thank you, come on Andi, we should check out the clothes section,' insisted Isla.

Flats paid for his supplies and took them out to his car. He sat patiently waiting with Jeeves for the two young women to come out. Eventually they emerged smiling and carrying a few bags.

'I finally bought myself a pair of wellies to wear in the garden,' said Andrea, 'and a new jacket ….. And a couple of nice tops.'

'Don't forget the new skirt,' reminded Isla.

'Oh yeh; I also got you a new scarf and we bought a couple of cakes for tea,' added Andrea.

'That's very kind of you, now let's go home. I have some work to do to protect my chickens.'

When they got back to the cottage, Jeeves leapt from the car and ran off barking furiously. Flats quickly followed to see what his dog was angry about. His heart skipped a beat when he saw the tail of a Fox disappear over the fence at the top of his garden. He tentatively approached his chicken house where his worse fears were realised, his beloved hens had been slaughtered and one had been taken.

'Oh no, that's awful. Why are Foxes so cruel?' asked Andrea as she caught up with Flats.

He put his arm around her shoulder; 'You can't entirely blame the Fox, it's probably a Vixen with young cubs and she's just doing what's needed to feed them.'

'How can you remain so calm and blasé about it? They were your chickens,' said Isla.

'Look, it's partly my fault for not making their enclosure strong enough. It's not the first time that this has happened, but trust me, it will be the last. I must build a stronger home for the next chickens. Now let's get the car unloaded and then I'll clear up this mess.'

Chapter Two

The week of the Cheltenham festival soon came around and Flats drove to his friend Reg's garage.

'Morning Flats, what can I do for you? Would you like me to fill your car with petrol to double its value?'

'Ha, ha; I will ignore that comment. I actually came to see if you wanted to go to Cheltenham on Friday. I have a spare pass given to me by Kenny Race, the trainer.'

'I didn't realize that you knew him, of course I would love to go. You know that I have a passion for horse racing, especially over the jumps. Thank you for asking me'

'That's settled then, come over to the cottage around eight and we can make a full day of it.'

'Is anyone else going or is it just a lad's day out?'

'The girls will be coming with us; it'll be the first time at a race meeting for either of them. Well I best get on, loads to do, see you Friday morning.' Flats then made his way across town, to the local builder's yard.

'Good morning sir, can I help you?' asked a cheery man in the yard.

'I hope so, I need a few breeze blocks and some bricks, oh and some sand and cement.'

'Certainly, do you know the exact quantities?'

'Yes I do; now where is that piece of paper? Ah, here it is, I need thirty breeze blocks, two hundred bricks, twelve bags of sand, four bags of cement and twenty brick ties. Tell me, when can you deliver this lot?'

'Come into the office and I'll check the delivery schedule ….. Now let me see, where do you live?'

Flats gave his address. 'That's nice and local, how does Wednesday morning grab you?'

'Perfect, thank you, now how much do I owe you?'

After paying for the supplies Flats headed home. When he walked into the kitchen, Andrea was on her knees scrubbing the floor. Jeeves ran over to her.

'Oh Jeeves, look at the mess you've made, your paws are dirty. Come here boy.' The dog duly obeyed and Andrea washed each of his paws before wiping over the floor again. 'Give me a minute and I'll pop the kettle on.'

'That's okay, I can do that. A quick cuppa and then I'm going to make a start on the new chicken enclosure.'

'I won't be much longer with the cleaning and then I can give you a hand. So what are you going to do different this time, in order to stop a Fox getting at our new chickens?'

'Well I can't do too much today but I need to dig out some footings. If we put them a couple of feet down into the ground and then build a few rows of bricks, a Fox won't be able to tunnel underneath them. The bricks and other supplies are arriving on Wednesday so I need to prepare the area.'

Out in the garden, Flats measured out the area for the footings. Andrea insisted on helping to dig out the soil even though Flats tried to persuade her that it was hard work. 'Are you trying to say that I'm too weak to wield a spade? I want to help and whilst we're on the subject of digging, when are we going to plant more vegetables?'

'Ooh get you, you're quite the country girl now,' teased Flats.

'You got that right pops, I love eating fresh veggies from our garden, and eggs from the shops simply don't taste as good as our own.'

Flats shook his head. 'That's enough of the 'pops' business too, you cheeky so and so.'

She could tell from the look on his face that it had amused him. Jeeves was parading back and forth along the boundary fence like a guard on patrol. Suddenly they heard the phone ring. 'I'll get it,' said Andi and off she went.

A few minutes later she returned. 'That was a Mr. Stirling Silva. He has just taken over a new warehouse in the town and wanted to know if you could advise him on the security he needs for it. I told him you could so he's coming here in an hour.'

'That's a bit different from our usual assignments, how did he find our number?'

'He said that you were recommended to him by Dave Higgins.'

Flats smiled, 'That's going to cost me some more raffle tickets next time I see him.'

Precisely one hour later, there was a knock on the door. After calming Jeeves down, Andrea answered it to find a man dressed casually but smart with it.

'Hello, I'm Stirling Silva, are you the young lady that I spoke to earlier?'

'Yes, that would be me, Andrea Magull, pleased to meet you. Won't you come in? Don't worry about the dog, he's been fed,' she quipped as she led the way to the sitting room.

As Stirling followed her he looked around; 'You have a charming home.'

Flats entered the room. 'Hello, you must be Mr. Silva I presume.'

'Yes I am for my sins,' he replied in a charming manner. 'You must be Mr. Flats Magull.'

The two men shook hands. 'Please, let's dispense with the formality, just call me Flats.'

'And you can call me Andi, would you like a cup of tea or coffee?'

'In that case, call me Stirling and yes, tea would be nice. Now that we have established who we are, I'll get straight to the point. As I told your delightful daughter; I have just taken over one of the new warehouses in Yeovil and need advice on security. It's going to be a Bonded Warehouse so it's paramount that the place is impenetrably secure at all times.'

'I see, exactly what do you want me to do?'

'I was reliably informed that you are one of the best authorities on crime detection, so I would like to hire you to oversee the installation of the alarm system and CCTV. The perimeter fencing has to be secure too.'

'That's quite a responsibility to undertake,' said Flats.

'Will you accept the challenge? I am prepared to meet your costs, no matter what they are. Money is no object for this project; it just has to be right, I'm sure you understand.'

Andrea poured them all some tea and offered a cup to Stirling. 'Help yourself to milk and sugar.'

'Okay Stirling, we will help you. Now when do you want us to start?' Flats asked after considering the request.

'As soon as possible please, I only have a month to get everything ready.'

'In that case, how are you fixed for tomorrow, say around ten?'

'Splendid,' said Stirling as he put down his cup, 'I look forward to seeing you in the morning, here's the address,' he added, handing over a card before leaving.

'Well that was a result, we have another job,' said

Andrea proudly. 'By the way, what is a Bonded Warehouse?'

'Are you aware that many goods brought into this country, such as cigarettes, perfume and alcohol are subject to import duty, which is a type of tax?'

'No I didn't; so what does that have to do with a Bonded Warehouse?'

'Well, if a company imports any of these types of goods, they can store them in a Bonded Warehouse and delay paying the duty until the goods are released from it. Take perfume for example; most of it is sold at either Valentine's Day or Christmas. No one wants to leave it to the last minute to import them, so they bring them in early and store them in such warehouses. Then as soon as it leaves for the distributors and shops, the duty becomes payable to the customs office.'

'Gotcha; Now, I understand. The need for security is obvious, and we have to make the place impregnable.'

'Yes Andi; that is exactly what we have to do and hopefully tomorrow you will learn what's required.'

When Isla came home after work Andrea couldn't wait to tell her about the security assignment.

'You're having more fun than I am,' she replied.

'Is police work becoming a bit mundane?' asked Flats.

'Not really, it's quiet more than mundane. It's all petty crimes at the moment, you know, the bread and butter cases, a car theft, some shop lifting, that sort of thing. Most of it's being handled by the beat Bobbies. They are in the process of installing the new communications desk for us to be able to use our two way radios though.'

'That should make it easier for you to catch criminals.'

'Yeh you're right, the most exciting aspect is over who will man, the new desk. Nick suggested WPC Knott but Hoskins is objecting, he thinks she is better employed elsewhere.'

'Well I'm glad I don't have to make that decision,' said Andrea. 'I like her, she's very clever.'

Flats nodded in agreement. 'You're right there Andi but being a local girl, she will know the area when it comes to directing any patrol car to a certain place. Now pipe down you two, it's time for the Archers.'

Chapter Three

The following morning Flats and Andrea headed for the industrial estate to meet with Mr. Silva.

'It's quite nice being driven for a change,' said Flats, 'This Escort is a nice motor, although Jeeves won't agree, he really doesn't like being in the back.'

As they approached the entrance to the warehouse site, Flats told Andrea to stop the car. 'Now then young lady, what is your first impression?'

'It's very big, in fact, much bigger than I thought it would be,' she replied.

'I was referring to the security aspect of the site. There is much work to do if Stirling expects to be operational in one month. Drive over there to the offices,' he directed whilst pointing out where she should go.

As Andrea parked the car, Stirling, accompanied by a smartly dressed woman, came out of the main warehouse to greet them. 'Good morning, Flats, Andi, meet Julie Noted, my personal assistant. So tell me, what are your first impressions?'

'The building itself is very impressive but forgive me for being blunt; who on earth designed this site? If someone from customs and excise inspects this place, they will condemn it immediately.'

'Oh dear, please don't say that, tell me what's wrong and I will have it remedied,' said Stirling worriedly.

'Okay; firstly, the perimeter fence is not high enough and the top two feet should be slanted inwards at 45 degrees. You should have razor wire all along the slanted part making a suitable deterrent for potential burglars. The posts supporting the wire need to be thicker and closer together.'

'Very good; are you taking this down Julie?'

'Yes Mr. Silva, every detail.'

'Let's consider the entrance next. Once again; forgive my being blunt, but what is that timber box doing there?'

'That's for the entry and exit guard so he doesn't get wet and has a seat,' replied Stirling in a concerned manner.

Flats looked him in the eye. 'How would you like to do a twelve hour shift stuck in that?'

'Ah well, we thought of that, there will be at least three guards on duty at all times and they will rotate their duties. One will be at the entrance; one will be by the offices and the third in the warehouse.'

Flats shook his head in disbelief. 'Picture this; I want to turn this place over, so I hire, or even steal a decent sized lorry and drive straight through the entrance. That wooden construction will not stop me. Just as importantly, why is there such a wide entrance?'

'We thought one side for Lorries coming in, and the other for going out,' replied Stirling.

Flats turned to Julie, 'Can I borrow your notepad please?'

'Yes of course,' she replied, handing it over.

They watched as Flats made a rough sketch. 'There now; that's what you need at the entrance. A security building built from bricks to include a toilet and facilities to make a brew. I would have two guards positioned in the security office at all times. Two entrances, one for cars and one for Lorries, the vehicles will come out the same way they entered. I also suggest that you have a fence erected between the car park and the building. Employees will have to enter the warehouse on foot.'

'That makes sense; it's so obvious when you point out these observations. What else?'

'Julie, can you go through the Yellow Pages and find three commercial fencing firms and three builders. Arrange for them to be here, on site, at 10 o'clock Thursday morning. We will be here to meet them and confirm exactly what is required; it doesn't hurt to create a bit of competition for work, and we'll scrutinize their tenders once they offer them up. Now shall we check out the main building and then the offices?' said Flats.

'I think I should have bought more raffle tickets from Dave. I owe him for putting me onto you,' said Stirling.

Flats stopped walking and turned to Andrea. 'If you were going to install CCTV, where would you suggest we place the cameras?'

'Okay ….. One above the door covering the entrance of the warehouse and one on each corner of the building. I think there should be another at the entrance by the security office and there needs to be a couple positioned to see the loading area with another at the entrance to the main offices.'

'I agree with you but I think we should also have a few more around the perimeter to spot any potential intruders. Any questions Stirling?'

'Only one, do you think we can get the work completed within a month?'

'I can't promise that, but we will have a damned good try. How are you getting on with your recruitment?'

'We start interviewing next week. Why do you ask?'

'Make sure they are thoroughly vetted; speak to Sergeant Hoskins at the main police station. Tell him that I sent you and he might be able to help with the background checks.'

'I think he'd get WPC Knott to help,' suggested Andrea.

'You're probably right. Well Stirling, Julie, we'll be on our way. See you both on Thursday, in the meantime, if you need me, give me a call.'

As they drove back to the cottage, Flats praised Andrea for her observations which made her feel very good inside. 'You did miss out a couple of places but we can add them next time. I didn't want to say anything in front of Stirling and Julie.'

'I'm still learning but today has opened my eyes as to why attention to detail is so important. I will be better prepared next time.'

'Andi my dear, this was your first time on such a job, don't be hard on yourself. When you do security work, you have to think like a criminal. Put yourself in their shoes and try to fathom out how you would break into the place in question.'

'Okay, I understand, in future I will try to be more cunning in my outlook.'

~~~~

The following day, the building materials were delivered as promised. 'Now we have to move all this to the site of the chicken house and begin work,' said Flats.

With Andrea's help, and after many trips using a wheelbarrow, everything was moved.

'What's our next job?' asked Andrea.

'There's a pile of old broken slabs and bricks in the top corner of the garden, we need to put them in the trench that we dug. I'll get a lump hammer to break some of it into smaller pieces.'

By the end of the day, the footings for the new chicken enclosure were finished. 'That's a good day's work, thanks for your help Andi.'

'No worries pops, it was hard but I enjoyed it, I think a good long soak in the tub is on the cards for me.'

'Oy you; Less of the pops,' he said smiling. 'A hot bath? Now that sounds like a good idea. I'm looking forward to Friday and our day at the races,' replied Flats, 'But first we have to take care of things at Stirling's new warehouse tomorrow. But for now, you take your bath and I'll walk Jeeves.'

It was precisely 10 o'clock on Thursday morning when Flats and Andrea arrived at the warehouse. 'It's probably best if we keep Jeeves on his lead, what with so many strangers about.'

'Okay, I'll keep him by me, but I want to be close to you so that I can learn how to handle the different people we will be dealing with.'

'If you're ready ….. Then let's get to it.'

Flats could see several men standing by the entrance to the offices but there was no sign of Stirling. 'Good morning gentlemen; which of you are the builders?'

Three men acknowledged him. 'If you would like to come with me please?' He turned to the others present, 'I assume you men must be representing the fencing companies, if you would kindly wait here, I won't be long.'

They walked across to the entrance where Flats wanted the security office built. He explained in great detail what he required and why.

'Excuse me sir,' enquired one of the men, 'Do you have a copy of the plans?'

'That's a very good question; I have to admit that I don't have any plans. You have the size of the building and you're aware that it will be a single storey. I've told you what will be required internally so that should be enough for you to formulate a close estimate. By the time the construction begins, you will have the plans. Now are there any questions?'

All of the men shook their heads and began assessing the site and making sketches. 'Very good, please have your quotes by Monday and let Mr. Silva have them. Talk of the devil, here he is now.'

After introducing himself to the men, he asked Flats how far he had got. 'I've just been giving the builders some instructions but have to admit that I forgot that they will need plans drawn up. Luckily I know an architect and he owes me a favour. Now I need to talk to the people from the fencing companies.'

'Okay, I will leave you to get on with that, if you need me, I'll be in my office,' said Stirling.

After giving the men a quick tour of the site, and explaining what was required, Flats went inside the office building where he found Stirling and Julie.

'We're done for the time being, you should receive the estimates by Monday and then you and I can go through them, if that's okay with you?'

'Of course; as you are aware, we are up against a tight schedule so the sooner we get started, the better.'

'Then if there's nothing else, I will go and see my architect friend right away. I'll give you a call later to confirm he is able to undertake this project and on that note, I'll bid you good day.'

Once they were in the car, Andrea asked about the plans. 'It goes to show how easy it is to forget something, but I'm sure my friend Les will come to the rescue.'

Flats drove to his friend's home. 'Wow! What an unusual house,' exclaimed Andrea.

'He designed it himself and had a little trouble getting the plans passed. Les would say that he's a visionary, whereas I, on the other hand, think he's eccentric. Either way, we have been friends for many years.'

Flats knocked on the door. Les was surprised to see him and cordially invited the two of them in. 'I assume that this young lady is your daughter, I had heard something on the grapevine.'

'Yes, this is Andrea.' She smiled and nodded at him.

'Pleased to meet you my dear, now what brings you here Flats?'

'Do you remember saying that you owe me a favour? Well, hopefuly, I've come to collect it.'

'That's fair enough, so what can I do for you?'

'I need some plans drawing.'

'Okay, you know that's my job, so what exactly is it that your wanting to build?'

'A security office for one of the new warehouses on the outskirts of town. There is however, a slight snag, I need them by Monday.'

'You don't want much, do you? Have you got the dimensions?'

'Yes I have ….. Somewhere.' Flats rifled through his pockets and produced a piece of paper with measurements on it. He then proceeded to give a description of what he wanted.

'I get you; I know exactly what you want. Lucky for you I have some plans for something very similar that I drew a couple of years ago. Give me a minute while I look them out.'

After checking through several drawers, Les found the drawings. 'Here you are, is this the sort of thing that you had in mind?'

Flats looked at the plans. 'That is almost perfect; the only thing missing is the high kerb around it.'

Andrea looked on silently, taking in every detail.

'As it's you and I owe you a favour, I will have your plans ready by midday on Monday,' informed Les.

'Splendid, I'll pop round and pick them up. Thanks Les.'

They left and headed back to the cottage. 'Would you like to call Stirling and let him know that everything is now in hand? Inform him that we will meet him around two in the afternoon on Monday after we've collected the plans.'

Chapter Four

Friday morning there was a scramble in the cottage to get ready for their day at the races. The excitement was palpable. Flats informed the young women that they should have a hearty breakfast before they left. 'The food at the race course will be very expensive.' As they sat and ate, he advised them that they should take warm coats, just in case the weather changes for the worst. Flats looked at his watch; 'Reg will be here soon,' he announced. Sure enough, a few minutes later Reg arrived in his Land Rover. 'I forgot to mention that we are going in Reg's motor today; apparently the parking at Cheltenham can be quite muddy at times and his vehicle can handle it.'

 He opened the door to let his friend in. 'Good morning Reg, are you feeling lucky?' asked Flats.

'Yeh, but I bought a spare shirt as a precaution.' His reply made the two men laugh but the girls looked puzzled. 'It's an old expression,' explained Flats, 'to lose your shirt means you have lost all your money; usually betting on a sure thing, hence the comment.'

As everyone was ready, they all got into the Land Rover and set off. Jeeves made himself comfortable on the back seat between Andrea and Isla. 'How far is it to Cheltenham?' asked Andrea.

'I'm not sure of the exact distance, but it will probably take a couple of hours,' replied Reg.

Flats had taken out a notepad and pencil to make some

notes regarding the job at the warehouse. 'I don't suppose you could avoid the bumps Reg; I'm trying to write here.'

It was approximately two hours before they arrived at the racecourse. Reg drove into the VIP entrance and once they had shown their passes, a course Marshall directed them to a parking spot. Flats asked him where he could find his friend Kenny Race.

'You should find him near the stables sir; his horse box is parked close to them.'

Flats thanked him and after putting Jeeves on his lead, he suggested they should go and say hello to their generous host. As they approached the horse box, Flats saw Kenny. 'Good morning,' he called.

'Hello Flats, it's good to see you, I'm so glad you made it. Now if my memory serves me right, you are …..
Andrea and this is Isla how are you both?'

'I'm very well thank you but I did say that you could call me Andi.'

'Yes, so you did, and who is this gentleman?'

'I'm Reg, a friend of Flats and a very avid racing fan. I've won a few bob backing your horses; especially Sir Basil,' how is he?'

'Come and see for yourself, he's just come back from his morning gallop.' They all followed Kenny to the stables where Sir Basil was being groomed.

'What a magnificent animal,' exclaimed Reg, 'he looks even better in the flesh. I've only seen him run on the television before.'

Flats held back whilst the others took a closer look at the horse. 'Don't worry about your dog,' encouraged Kenny, 'he's used to seeing them around the stables back at our yard.'

After they had inspected Sir Basil, Kenny pointed to a tent. 'That's one of the sponsors, flash your passes and you can enjoy some free hospitality. I'll catch up with you all a bit later.'

'This day is getting better by the minute,' said Reg.

'I don't understand why you're so excited, you don't drink,' commented Flats.

'Maybe not, but I like to eat,' replied Reg with a wink.

As they entered the tent, Flats handed his dog's lead to Andrea. 'Get me a pint of real ale please Reg; if they have any, I'll nip off and get us some race programs.'

He returned a few minutes later and handed out a

program to each of them as Reg gave him his beer. 'Now you can pick the horses you want to have a 'flutter' on; That's slang for placing a bet by the way,' he explained.

'How do we bet? I've never done this before,' said Andrea blushing at her naivety.

Isla sidled up to her. 'You're not the only one; I've never done this before either.'

Reg stepped in and gave them a quick brief of what to do. 'On page four is the list of runners for the first race. Have a look at what you fancy and then check out the odds; for instance, Mayflower is the current favourite. If you check the boards over there you will see it's currently priced at 4/1. That means if you bet one pound and it wins, you win four pounds, plus you get your original pound stake back.'

'I see, and what happens if it doesn't win?' asked Isla.

'You lose your pound,' replied Reg.

'I like the name of this one, 'The Cottager,' said Andrea.

'Well it might have a fancy name but it doesn't stand much chance, it's an outsider, with current odds of 33/1.'

'That means I win thirty three pounds if it wins,' replied Andrea excitedly.

'You have more chance backing a donkey on Weston Super Mare beach,' replied Reg cheekily.

'Well I'm going to have a ….. What did you call it; A flutter? And put ten shillings on it,' said Andrea defiantly. Isla also liked the name of the horse and decided to copy her friend's selection. Flats picked out his choice whilst Reg backed the favourite. After placing their bets, they continued to enjoy the free refreshments until it was time for the first race. Almost everyone in the tent went outside to get a view of the course. The place was packed tight but Andrea was fascinated by the bookmakers. She didn't understand their jargon but that only increased her excitement and expectations. She pointed to the first race details in her program. 'Reg, could you please explain what all of this means?'

'Of course; the first number there is the distance, which is just over two miles. Then it tells you that it's a hurdle race, basically over the jumps or fences. The next item tells you that the going is good to soft. Some horses prefer the ground to be hard whereas some prefer it soft.'

Isla had moved closer and was observing and listening intently. 'What do all the other things mean?' she asked.

'The numbers and letters on the left tell you how the horse has performed recently. P means it was pulled up; F means it fell; U tells you the horse unseated its rider; 0

means it was unplaced whereas 1 to 4 is where they were placed. The next part you know because that's the name of the horse; under each one is the name of the trainer and then the colours, or silks as they are known, that the jockey will wear, and finally, the name of the jockey who will ride the horse.'

They were interrupted by the Tannoy announcing that the horses were coming under starter's orders. All eyes turned to the course; 'AND THEY'RE OFF,' came the cry from the huge megaphones. The crowd began to cheer and urge on the horses as they approached the first fence. All of the horses cleared the hurdle and charged towards the second. Andrea turned to Isla, 'Oh dear, our poor horse is almost last.'

Flats put his hand on her shoulder and in a reassuring voice told her; 'Don't despair, there's still a long way to go, he might improve.'

As the race continued, the volume of noise increased and was reaching a crescendo as the horses entered the home straight. They were now strung out with just three close together at the front, including 'The Cottager'.

Andrea and Isla were now screaming their heads off as they called out its name. Then came the unthinkable, the front three cleared the penultimate hurdle and 'The Cottager' landed in front. From that moment there was no catching him and he began to pull away from the other two. Over the last, and he was now a few lengths in front with the margin increasing with every stride. The two girls were jumping up and down as they cheered the winner home. Reg could not believe his eyes, his horse, the favourite, was well beaten and finished fourth. 'There's just no logic to explain that,' he uttered shaking his head in disbelief.

Flats suggested that they return to the sponsor's tent until the next race. Andrea wanted to soak up the atmosphere of the occasion and with Isla, watched the hustle and bustle around them.

'We should check the runners for the next race,' suggested Isla.

Inside the tent, Flats was supping a complimentary ale and chatting with Reg when a rather flustered Kenny came rushing up to him; 'Flats, you are not going to believe me, but I think that Sir Basil has been stolen.'

'That's ridiculous, it's not possible,' exclaimed Reg, 'we all saw him earlier.'

'What makes you think he's been taken?' asked Flats.

'I went to his allocated stable with Willie, his jockey, and it was empty. We have checked all the other stables but there's no sign of him. You must help me Flats, I need your expertise to find him, the owners will be extremely irate when I tell them.'

'Calm down Ken, there must be a reasonable explanation, let's go and take a look,' offered Flats.

They all walked to the stabling area where they could see Sir Basil's name over one of the doors. A puzzled looking jockey was standing by it.

'This is Willie Wynne who is supposed to be riding him in the Gold Cup and here is where Sir Basil should be,' informed Kenny.

'Who was the last person to see the horse?'

'That would have been us two; he was tethered outside his stable.'

Willie's face dropped and he went bright red.

Flats noticed the forlorn expression. 'Do you know something that you would like to tell us?'

'I had just given Sir Basil his little treat, a sherbet lemon, and was about to put him back into the stable when one of the yard lads offered to do it for me. As I needed to use the toilet, I thought that it couldn't do any harm, and left him to it. I'm so sorry Mr. Race.'

Kenny gave him an angry stare and was about to lay into the poor jockey, when Flats intervened. 'Hang on Ken; Willie, can you describe this lad?'

'Yes of course, he's about five foot nine, ginger hair ….. THAT's HIM,' yelled Willie, pointing to a young lad.

'Excuse me,' called Flats, 'can I have a word?'

The young lad walked over to them. 'What can I do for you sir,' he said politely.

'We are looking for the horse that should be in this stable, which you offered to attend to, do you know where it is now?'

'He should be in the parade ring; I was about to lead him inside the stable when one of the course clerks gave me half a crown to take him to the ring. He told me that it would save him a job as he was busy.'

'Who did you give the horse to?' demanded Kenny.

'I don't know his name, he was wearing a suit and looked official; he even had a pass pinned to his lapel.'

Flats looked at Kenny. 'Have you checked the parade ring to see if Sir Basil is there?'

'See for yourself, there are no horses, they are not due

for another ….. ooh ten minutes or so,' replied Kenny looking at his watch.

'You had better inform the owners and the officials, and call the police,' instructed Flats.

As Kenny trudged off, Flats informed his party that he would need to make some enquiries immediately. Isla offered to help and asked where they should start. 'There's quite a few people milling around here, so if you would like to start at the far end of the stabling block, I'll begin from here and we'll meet in the middle.'

'What would you like me to do?' asked Andrea.

'You're with me of course.'

'I can help to,' said Reg, 'I'll go and have a word with the men at the entrance and exit to the course. To move a horse would have needed a decent sized vehicle, one of them would surely have seen it leave if that be the case.'

Chapter Five

After an exhaustive questioning of everyone in the stabling area; Flats and Isla were comparing notes when Reg returned. 'According to the men at the exit, two horseboxes have left the course since the races began. They don't check vehicles as they leave, but the men told me that they're sure one of them was a Blue Bedford and the other was a Green horsebox but couldn't remember the make of it.'

'That's good work Reg, but it doesn't help us that much, unfortunately.'

'I have spoken to several people and a few of them have confirmed that they saw the ginger haired lad leading Sir Basil towards the show ring,' informed Isla.

'My information was exactly the same. Nobody pays much attention to a horse being led through this area. After all, it's not like that's an unusual occurrence. Isla; would you mind finding the ginger haired lad and getting a description of the man he handed Sir Basil to?'

'Of course, leave it with me.' Andrea said that she would go with her to help spot the young man.

Willie came back to the stabling block looking very downhearted. 'I've been sacked,' he informed them.

'That's harsh, but you can understand the reason why. Let me give you my number, just in case you remember anything that might help us find the horse,' said Flats.

Shortly afterwards, a dejected Kenny came up to Flats, 'The owners are extremely angry, they have threatened to remove their other horses from my stables, if I don't find Sir Basil, this could ruin me. They have called the police but I told them that I also wanted to engage you. If you can find him I will make it worth your while, I promise.'

'I will do my best. You said 'owners' are there more than one of them?'

'Yes, it's a syndicate led by a Seamus Finnegan and they are known as the 'Shamrock group.' As far as I know, there are five members.'

'Can you get me all of their names and any addresses that you know? We have to start somewhere and that's as good a place as any.'

By this time, rumours were spreading all around the course that the favourite for the Gold Cup was missing. Many punters were angry as they had already laid out money on the favourite and were demanding that their wagers be returned. An announcement over the Tannoy called for calm but it wasn't until the police arrived a few minutes later, that the crowd began to quieten down. Andrea and Isla returned with smug grins on their faces. 'I have a good description of the man who took the horse off our ginger haired lad but clever clogs here had a bright idea. Go on, you tell him,' urged Isla.

'While Isla was making notes, I was looking around and noticed the TV cameras and thought; maybe they caught something on film that could help us.'

'Well done Andi, that's an excellent bit of detection.'

A policeman approached Flats and wanted to know who he was. Isla intervened, 'I'm DS White from Yeovil and we are here as guests of trainer Kenny Race. This gentleman is Mr. Flats Magull, an ex-detective, and between us, we have begun making enquiries.'

'Thank you for that, please wait while I fetch my boss, I'm sure he will want to speak to you.'

A few minutes later, the officer returned accompanied by two other men. 'These are the people that I told you about sir.'

'Thank you constable, you can return to your duties,'

said one of the men. 'Now then, which one of you ladies is the DS?'

'That would be me sir, DS White from Yeovil branch.'

'I'm Chief Inspector Godwin and this is Sergeant Best, Cheltenham station. I understand that you have already made some preliminary enquiries, would you mind filling us in on what you've found so far.'

'Certainly Chief; this is Flats Magull and his daughter Andrea. They are private investigators and this is their friend Reg. As soon as Mr. Race informed us that Sir Basil had gone missing, we spoke to as many people as we could find in the stabling area. Unfortunately, we haven't found any significant information. We do, however; have a description of the gentleman who allegedly led the horse to the show ring. Reg was told by the marshals that only two Lorries have left the site since the racing began.'

'That's good work, would you please give my Sergeant the description of the gentleman in question. We will take over from here, thank you for your assistance.'

'A moment Chief, if you will; Kenny Race has engaged me to find his missing horse, so I would appreciate being kept informed of any findings. In return, I will let you know of anything that we find,' said Flats.'

'That's fair enough, but any information that we pass on will go through official channels to DS White at her station. I bid you good day, I have work to do. Okay Sergeant, assign some men to make a list of all the horseboxes on site and find their owners. Then see if you can establish who sent their vehicle off site and why.'

'What are we going to do now?' asked Andrea.

'I suggest you make your choice for the next race as it will be starting very soon. In the meantime, I need to speak to Kenny.'

He found his friend being interviewed by a policeman. 'Excuse me officer, this is the P.I. that I told you about and I think he may want to speak to me.'

'Right you are sir, we're just about done here so I'll leave you to it, but we may need to speak to you again.'

'Kenny, tell me who dishes out the passes for the festival?' asked Flats.

'Mine came automatically when my horses were entered for the festival, but I believe they are sent from the booking office. We should ask Dennis, he's the course clerk and he's bound to know,' replied Kenny.

After a short search, they located Dennis who was looking very perturbed. 'This is the first time anything

43

like this has ever happened at the festival. I could lose my job over this,' he told them.

'Dennis, this is my good friend and P.I. Flats Magull, he would like to ask you a couple of questions.'

'Do you keep a record of who the VIP passes are sent out to? And are there any details kept of the vehicles that are permitted entry?'

'We do record the passes, if you check yours you will notice it is numbered, but we don't register the vehicles. Many owners have more than one horsebox and don't decide until the day which to use.'

'Would it be possible to have a copy of pass numbers and who received them?'

'Yes of course, I'll go and organise that with my secretary right away. Where shall I find you?'

'We will be in the sponsor's tent,' replied Flats. 'Now then Kenny, have you got the list of the horse's owners?'

'If you can drop by my stables tomorrow I will have it ready for you.'

'Okay, if I don't see you again today, then I'll see you in the morning around ten.'

Flats returned to the sponsor's tent but almost everyone was outside cheering on the horses in the second race. He could hear the excitable screams coming from Andrea and Isla. 'God forbid if they've picked another winner,' he muttered to himself.

Reg came into the tent with a forlorn look of disbelief etched across his face. 'They've done it again, 14/1 outsider and it has just romped home. Do you have a spare set of darts ….. Or a pin?'

Flats couldn't resist a wry smile as the two girls bounced into the tent grinning like Cheshire cats. 'Tonight's tea is on us, fish and chips from the local chippy,' they said in unison.

A woman approached Flats, 'Are you Mr. Magull?'

'Yes, that's me, can I help you?' She handed him an envelope, 'I was asked to give you this; it's a list of all the passes and their recipients.'

Flats thanked the woman as she left. Before he could take a look inside; Sergeant Best approached him. 'We've found a Blue horsebox abandoned a few miles away and the Chief wanted to know if you would like to take a look.'

'That's very good of him; yes I would like to see it. Reg,

can I borrow your motor?'

'No need for that my friend, I'm coming with you.'

The girls looked at each other and nodded. 'We're coming too.'

'Give me a minute please Sergeant and I'll be with you.' He took the lead from Andrea and walked with his dog to Sir Basil's stable. 'Okay boy, find.'

They watched as Jeeves had a good sniff around the stable and followed him as he padded away. A short distance from the stable, he stopped and barked. 'Well done boy. This is where the horse was led into a vehicle,' he declared.

Flats pointed to some tyre tracks, 'This is your domain Reg, can you remember these marks?'

'I reckon so,' he replied as he studied the tread pattern.

'Do you think this is important?' asked Isla pointing to the ground.

'Sergeant, do you have an evidence bag please?'

'As a matter of fact, I do,' he replied as he pulled one out of his jacket pocket.

Flats carefully retrieved the remains of a cigar and sealed

it in the bag. 'Do you think that may be important sir?'

'I'm not sure Sergeant, but as it's at the scene of what we perceive to be the crime, it might be. Now let's go and look at this abandoned horsebox.'

Chapter Six

Reg followed the Chief inspector's car to where the Lorry had been left. As they parked, a patrol car pulled up behind them. Before anyone could check out the vehicle, Flats suggested letting Jeeves go first. The Chief Inspector agreed, 'Okay boy off you go.'

They all watched as Jeeves thoroughly sniffed the ground and as he approached the tail gate, he began to bark furiously. 'I think we can conclude that the horse was moved in this vehicle.' He turned to Reg, 'What do you make of the tyre pattern?'

'That certainly matches those made back at the racecourse,' he confirmed. 'If you look at the other imprints by the tailgate, my guess is they belong to a trailer of sorts, probably a horsebox being towed by a car.'

'This heist was obviously very carefully planned,' observed the Chief.

Flats walked around the stranded Lorry whilst casting his eye over it. At the front of the vehicle, he caught Isla's attention and made a nodding gesture at the windscreen. At first she wasn't sure what she was looking for until Andrea whispered to her. She reached into her bag and took out a pen and a piece of paper; she glanced back at Flats and touched her nose before making a note.

Reg was studying the new tyre marks and suggested that the car used was most likely a Jaguar. 'If it's not one of them, then it's something very similar, certainly a large saloon.'

'Well done Reg, at least that narrows things down slightly.' He then noticed something on the ground. 'I need a distraction,' he whispered.

His friend didn't need to be told twice and he walked to the back of the Lorry. 'Do any of you officers have a camera?' he asked. 'It's probably a good idea to get some pictures of the area, especially the tyre marks.'

This was just enough time for Flats to remove his

handkerchief and pick up something from the ground. He moved towards Isla, 'Can you make a note of the registration?'

'Already done; is there anything else that I should note?'

He shook his head, 'I want to have a quick look in the back of the Lorry and then we can go.'

As he peered into the vehicle, the Chief was curious as to what he was looking for. 'I'm not really sure ….. May I take a closer look?'

'Be my guest, I don't think this vehicle is going to be much use to us. We are virtually certain the horse was removed from the course in it. I'm more interested in finding the vehicle used to take the animal from here.'

Something caught Flats' eye, 'Do you have a spare evidence bag please?'

'What have you found?' asked the Chief.

'It's probably nothing but there's a horse shoe on the floor and I'd like to bag it.'

'As far as I'm concerned, you can keep it. I don't intend to play the handsome Prince and try it on all horses in the area,' said the Chief sarcastically.

Once the horse shoe was in a bag, Flats announced that he and his friends would be leaving. 'I hope to be speaking to you soon, when one of us finds the horse.'

The police were cordoning off the area around the Lorry as Reg drove away. 'I assume that you would like to head for home.'

'Yes please Reg; sorry to cut your day short ladies, but I have work to do.'

'Don't you mean 'we' have work to do?' said Andrea. 'And what did you pick up off the ground?'

'There was another cigar butt and I believe it's the same brand as the one at the racecourse. 'I'm sure Dicky will be able to tell me.'

'That's a decent clue if they are the same brand,' said Isla, 'too much of a coincidence perhaps?'

'Exactly, and now we also have the pass number used to gain access to the course. What we need to figure out is where would one take and hide a prized stallion?'

They arrived back at the cottage and Reg dropped them off. 'See you around Flats and thanks for today.'

'And our thanks to you Reg, you have been most helpful. Right then, I need to call Dicky to see if he's in; any chance one of you could stick the kettle on?'

After making a quick call, Flats announced that his friend was home. 'I'll have a quick cuppa and then pop round to see him.'

Isla decided to stay home, so they left Jeeves with her, and Andrea drove Flats to Dicky's place. 'Come in, kettles on. Now what do you need my assistance with?'

Flats produced an evidence bag and unfurled his handkerchief. 'I would like to get your opinion on these two; do you think they are the same brand?'

'Give me a minute to get some gloves and a magnifying glass ….. Now let's have a look ….. Well for starters, I can tell you that they are King Edward cigars.' He then examined them a bit closer for several minutes. 'These cigars were smoked by the same person; I would stake my reputation on it.'

'How can you be so sure?' asked Andrea.

'Take a close look at the ends; both have been snipped by a cigar cutter. It's a common practice for the more discerning gentlemen. The one used on these is either too small, or the blade has a slight chip, hence the small tearing. So Flats, what is this all about?'

'We are investigating the disappearance of a horse from

the Cheltenham race course. Right in the middle of the day's racing.'

'You don't mean Sir ….. What's his name, the favourite for the gold cup?'

'Yes I do, and its name is Sir Basil, trained by Kenny Race. Do you know him?'

'Vaguely, I did hear on the news about it. I would offer my services but I am not sure how I could be of any use.'

'You have already been a great help. How we find the horse is another matter, it could be anywhere by now.'

'There has to be a reason as to why they stole this particular animal. If it's that valuable, my guess would be that someone wants it for breeding ….. Or ransom.'

'That's something we have to work out my friend, so we should be going, I have much to consider pertaining to this case. If I do require your services, I'll call you.'

Back at the cottage, Isla informed them that she had called the station to request a check on the Lorry's registration. 'That's a good idea but my hunch is that it was stolen. You would have to be very stupid to use your own vehicle to steal a horse,' said Flats

'I didn't think of that; but I have been busy. The pass in

the windscreen was issued to a Mr. Dara Nolan. I have asked Knotty to run some background checks for me.'

'Well done, that's great work; at least we now have a suspect. Changing the subject; are we still having fish and chips for tea?'

'Yes, we did promise you that,' answered Isla.

'Come on, I'll drive,' said Andrea picking up her keys.

Once the girls had left, Flats took Jeeves for a walk. As he strolled down the lane, he pondered on the idea that the horse was taken for breeding purposes. A thought crossed his mind, 'that's it' he thought.

When the girls returned from the chippie, he told them of his theory. 'Dicky's suggestion of breeding from Sir Basil is very logical. They could collect his sperm and impregnate any horse, no one would be any the wiser. We need to research stud farms and professional stables because they would have the technology and knowhow required.'

Chapter Seven

The following morning, Flats and Andrea headed for Kenny's racing stables while Isla went to work. 'I'll see if the Chief will allow us to borrow a couple of officers to help with your search.'

When they arrived, there were a couple of horseboxes parked near the stables and a few cars. Kenny came to meet them. 'This is the result of yesterday's tragic occurrence; the Shamrock Group are removing all of their horses. Happily, I can now take Willie back to ride for me; it was this lot that insisted upon sacking him.'

'Have you got the list of the group members for me?'

Kenny reached into one of his pockets. 'There you are; two of them are here now. The one over there with the hat is Dara Nolan, and that's his car the Brown Zodiac, and the guy with the sheepskin coat is Seamus Finnegan, he owns the Jensen.'

'Do you know where they are taking their horses?'

'Not sure, but I thought I heard one of them mention Wellington. If that's the case, they'll be going to Pete Holt's yard; he's the only trainer I know out that way.'

Flats started walking towards the stables. As he got closer he noticed that the Zodiac had a tow bar fitted. 'Excuse me for a minute Kenny; I would like to take a few pictures of Sir Basil's stall.'

'Be my guest, if you think it will help the investigation.'

Andrea followed Flats to the car. 'Use my camera to photograph the stable and discreetly take some pictures of their Lorries and cars, especially the rear ends. Leave Jeeves here, it will be easier without him.'

As they headed back to the stables, Flats noticed Seamus light up a cigar. 'That's a decent looking smoke, what brand is it?'

'King Edward, nothing but the best. Here, would you like to try one?'

'I don't normally smoke during the day; would you think it rude of me if I took one to enjoy later when I listen to the archers?'

'Not at all, help yourself. Seamus Finnegan, at your service.'

'Flats Magull, pleased to meet you. Was it your horse that was stolen yesterday?' he asked innocently.'

'Yes it was; are you a racing fan?'

'Sort of, I was at Cheltenham when Sir Basil was taken. I'm a good friend of Kenny's. He's hired me to find the horse, I'm a private investigator.'

The words caused a brief change in Seamus' expression which both Flats and Andrea noticed.

'I wish you good luck with your search; our syndicate would like to get our horse back.'

'Don't you fret sir, if anyone can find him, it's my dad, and he's the best in the business.'

'Well it was nice meeting you Flats; I need to speak to my partner, enjoy the cigar.'

When Seamus was out of earshot, Flats quietly spoke to Andrea, 'You're a crafty one, that comment made him a little uncomfortable and didn't go down too well. He wasn't best pleased to know why I'm here, well done.'

The last of the horses was loaded onto a Lorry and they left. 'Did you manage to get all the pictures?'

Andrea nodded, 'Everyone as you asked.'

Kenny was by the stable and had been joined by Willie. 'I nearly forgot, do you have a picture of Sir Basil?'

'I can get you one, give me a moment.'

'How are you feeling Willie?'

'I'm disappointed that I won't get to ride Sir Basil again, he's a lovely horse to ride, but at least I still have my job. If you do find him, make sure you have some Sherbet Lemons and give him one for me.'

Kenny came back and gave Flats a couple of photographs. 'What a good looking animal. Tell me how much do you really know about this Shamrock Group?'

'They're a bunch of Irishmen who, as well as having their fingers in many pies, enjoy their racing and own many horses. I believe they own a stable in Ireland. Why do you ask?'

'My gut feeling tells me that they know something about the disappearance of their horse. Anyway, we should get going, I'll be in touch.'

Back in the car, Andrea asked if he really believed that the syndicate was involved in the abduction. 'Let's just say it's beginning to look that way,' he answered as he nonchalantly studied the cigar he'd been given.

'Who would have thought that something like a discarded cigar end could be so important? But why kidnap your own horse?'

'That, my dear girl, is what we have to find out. Drive

straight to the police station if you would.'

Sergeant Hoskins greeted them warmly as usual. 'I hear you had an eventful day at the races. There was a lot of controversy surrounding yesterday's racing. The favourite from the first race was nobbled, as were a couple of the others. I understand they found traces of Xylazine in their blood samples.'

'That's a type of tranquilizer used as a calming agent.'

'How do you know that Andi,' queried the Sergeant.

'Well Sarge, this gal is a qualified pharmacist; I did learn something in my studies.'

'Did you learn how to be cheeky or did that come naturally?' he replied with a smile. 'Go on through Flats, the Chief is in his office.'

'Hello Flats, this is an unexpected surprise, come in, you too Andrea ..... And bring Jeeves.'

'Has Isla filled you in on my latest investigation? We've come to ask for some assistance.'

'Yes she did, and as we are a little quiet, thankfully, I told her to grab a couple of officers. Was there something else?'

'As a matter of fact there is, I have the names of a syndicate known as the Shamrock Group. They own the horse that was abducted during yesterday's racing. My gut feeling tells me that one or more of them may be involved, or at least know something about it.'

'You need to speak to Hoskins; he's very knowledgeable about horse racing. DS White is in the incident room where I believe she has roped in the Inspector to assist.'

'Thanks Larry, I appreciate your help.' He turned to Andrea, 'Would you give this list of names to Isla please; while I go and speak to Hoskins.'

'Ah Sarge, I've come to pick your brains. A little bird tells me that you are an authority on horse racing. What do you know about the Shamrock Group?'

He took a sharp intake of breath; 'Ooh now then ….. It's a group of Irishmen, six in total and was started by a Seamus Finnegan. They are all wealthy and share a love of racing, particularly over the jumps. Apart from the horse that was stolen, they own many others. It's not easy to determine how many because they buy and sell horses all the time. A couple of them jointly own a stable in Ireland and it's rumoured they have another somewhere on mainland Europe. Their racing stock is trained at several different stables throughout the country. You don't want to cross them; According to the grapevine they are involved in some illegal activities like race fixing, but nothing has been proven to date. If you're getting involved with them, my advice is to tread carefully.'

'Thank you Sarge, I'll bear that in mind. Do you know of any stud farms within a fifty mile radius of Cheltenham or where I might find such information?'

'I would think the Jockey Club is your best bet, excuse the pun, they at least should have a list of regulated breeders.'

Andrea joined them. 'Hey Sarge, I need a favour,' she grovelled cheekily. 'I have a few registration numbers that need checking, please.'

'I thought you were only taking pictures of the vehicles.'

'Isla's not the only one who carries a notebook and pen you know. I always have one to hand these days.'

'Well Sarge, what do you reckon?' asked Flats.

'How can anyone say no to her, I bet she's even got you wrapped around her little finger? Give me the list young lady and I'll see what I can do.'

'We'd better go and see if Isla and her team have made any progress, catch you later Sergeant.'

'Hello Flats, nice to see you again,' said Nick when he saw him enter the room.

'Hi Nick, thanks for helping us, have you got anything for me?'

'Until a few minutes ago, we only knew two of the members of the Shamrock Group; Seamus Finnegan and Dara Nolan. They are an interesting couple of characters to say the least. According to our information, these two own an abattoir and meat processing plant which is in a bit of financial trouble. Neither of them has much in their bank accounts and their houses are mortgaged to the hilt.'

'That's excellent work; I'm guessing WPC Knott had something to do with uncovering that information.'

'It's not just me, the others have played their part, especially DS White,' quipped WPC Knott.

'If you give us another day, we'll have more information regarding the rest of the group,' informed Isla. 'You don't need to hang around, I can fill you in later when I get home,' she added.

'It would seem Andi, that you and I are surplus to requirements, shall we go?'

Chapter Eight

Later that evening, Isla returned from her shift at the station. 'We're getting on well with our background checks; even the Chief has taken an interest. It seems that although there are six members, that we know of in the syndicate, they operate in pairs. You know about messrs Finnegan and Nolan but it seems that Aidan Lynch and Sean Kelly own a chain of restaurants called Dublin Fayre, and a couple of up market hotels. We don't have financial checks on them yet, or the last two, Messrs O' Donnell and Whelan, who have a couple of car dealerships. By the way, the Chief gave me a message for you, the radio system goes live on Monday and unless anything urgent comes in, we can carry on helping you find the horse.'

'As Andi and I have a meeting scheduled for Monday, do you think that someone could find out what stud farms are within fifty miles of Cheltenham? The Sergeant seems to think that the Jockey Club may have a list of them. If the weatherman is accurate, tomorrow is going to be a nice day so it's time Vinnie and me got re-acquainted.' The two young ladies looked at each other with puzzled expressions. 'Who is Vinnie?'

'Not 'who' ladies, but more of a 'what'. You'll have to wait until tomorrow to find out. Now do either of you fancy going to the pub for a drink?'

~~~~

Sunday morning, Flats was up early. He took Jeeves for a walk and decided to work on the new hen house. Andrea came out with a cup of tea.

'Would you like me to give you a hand?'

'I'm not sure what you can do, unless of course you can lay bricks. If you have nothing better to do, you could give me a hand with Vinnie when I've finished here.'

'Perhaps if you told what this Vinnie is, I would know what to do.'

'Let me finish these last few bricks and I'll show you.' She patiently watched as he laid the last couple of bricks. 'There, not much more to do and then we can get our new chickens, I miss the fresh eggs, don't you?' After cleaning his tools, he led her to the garage.

'Do you realize that in all the time I've been here, this will be the first time that you've allowed me to come in here?'

At the back of the garage she could see a tarpaulin

covering something. Flats began to remove it to reveal a large motorcycle. 'This is 'Vinnie', it's a Vincent Rapide and it goes like the name suggests, very quick.'

'Wow! It looks amazing; will you take me on it? I've never been on a motorcycle before.'

'We'll need to get you a helmet, a suitable leather jacket and some proper boots. Then I'll be happy to take you for a ride. Firstly though, it needs a good clean and a bit of maintenance before it goes out on the road.'

'Let me go and put on some old clothes and get a couple of rags, then I'll be happy to help clean it.'

Andrea went back in doors to find Isla sat at the kitchen table. After telling her about Vinnie, she went to her room and changed appropriately.

'Give me ten minutes and I'll come and lend a hand,' offered Isla. 'I love motorbikes.'

The three of them spent a couple of hours polishing the motorbike from top to bottom. Flats cleaned out the fuel system and finally announced that it was time to start the engine. After just two attempts on the kick-starter, it belched smoke and a flame as it roared into life.

'Blimey, it's very loud,' shouted Andrea. 'I can't wait to have a go on it.'

Flats turned off the choke and allowed the engine to idle happily. 'Tomorrow when we are in town, we'll go to a motorcycle shop and get you kitted out. We'll take him out for a spin when you're sorted.' He switched off the engine and for the rest of the day, Flats pottered around in the garden, and with help from Andrea; they planted some seeds and weeded the flower beds. 'I think Jeeves will need washing, look at the state of his paws,' observed Andrea.

The following morning, as Isla left for the station, Flats informed her that they would drop by to see her later in the day. 'Hopefully you will have some news for us.'

When Andrea was ready, she and Flats went into town in the new car. Jeeves was becoming accustomed to sitting on the back seat. Whilst Andrea drove, Flats began to fiddle with the controls of the police radio. It crackled into life but they didn't hear any voices. 'It must be quiet again,' he suggested. 'You need to take the next left.'

Andrea followed his instruction, 'Left again Andi and you'll see the motorcycle shop. Jeeves can wait in the car whilst we get what you need.'

When they entered the premises, Flats made straight for the helmet section. Andrea was mesmerized by the number of motorbikes for sale and stopped a few times to admire various models. 'Have a good rummage and decide which you prefer the look of. I would suggest a full face option, like these in this rack. You may feel a little claustrophobic at first, but you'll soon get accustomed to it, and they are by far the safest.'

'I like this one; it's very similar to yours.'

Flats beckoned to an assistant. 'We would like one of these to fit the young lady please.' After trying on a couple of them, they found one that fitted perfectly.

'They are much heavier than I thought they would be,' said Andrea viewing herself in a mirror, 'but it looks nice. What's next?'

'You need a jacket and some boots; could you help us young man?'

'Of course sir, the ladies clothing section is just over here. What size shoes do you take madam?'

'I'm a size five,' she replied. After choosing a pair of boots and a leather jacket, the assistant suggested that she might like some proper gloves. Eventually, with all the new attire purchased, they returned to the car. 'Will I need special trousers?' asked Andrea as she considered her new look.

'No, but I would definitely buy a good quality pair of Denim jeans.' Flats drove to the town centre where

Andrea went into a clothing shop and eventually emerged with a satisfied smile. 'When we get home, you will have to put some 'dubbing' on your jacket, gloves and boots. It's to protect the leather and make it waterproof, to a fashion. Now let's go and see if Les has drawn up the plans.' It didn't take long before they arrived at the architect's house.

'You are very prompt, come in, I have your plans here in my office. There you are, what do you think?'

'Very good Les, thank you, they're perfect. Send your bill to Mr. Silva. Andi can you give Les the address.'

'Here you are, I had it ready,' she replied handing over a piece of paper.

'That's not necessary; I did them to repay a favour.'

'Look my friend, that's between us, Mr. Silva doesn't know so send him a bill,' said Flats with a wink. 'Talking of which, we need to visit him next, come on Andi, no peace for the wicked.'

They said goodbye and headed for the warehouse.

Stirling was in his office, 'We're a little early but hopefully you have the quotes,' enquired Flats.

He picked up his phone; 'Julie, would you bring in the

folders containing the quotes please? Unfortunately Mr. Magull, you will see that only two of the fencing companies have responded.'

Julie entered with the folders; 'Pass them to Mr. Magull please.'

Flats looked at the fencing quotes first and compared them. 'There's very little to choose between them but this one looks a little more professional in its presentation and they can start at the end of the week.' He gave the document to Stirling and then checked out the builders quotes. Andrea was looking at them and trying to make some sense of it all. Flats moved one folder closer to her, 'See this; they can't start for two weeks whereas this one can start tomorrow. What does that tell you?'

'One of them is either desperate or not very good, which is why they can start immediately.'

'Very good, and when you compare that one with the third quote, neither of them can give a completion date.' After a thorough look through the folder, Flats passed another document to Stirling. 'I think this is the company we should go with, although they can't start right away, everything else looks pretty good. If you're in agreement, can I use a phone to ring them?'

'I am happy to accept you're judgement. We can do better than that; Julie would you contact this firm and then patch the call through to me. You can take the call here in my office.'

A couple of minutes later, the phone buzzed. Stirling picked up the phone and then handed it to Flats. 'Hello to you ….. We've looked at your quote for the security office and I just have a couple of questions …... Can you guarantee it will be finished within five weeks? ….. I see, yes I have the plans here ….. Is there any chance you can start a bit earlier than what you put in your quote? Okay, I will drop them off to you in the next hour. Bye for now. That's a stroke of luck; he has a couple of men who can start on the groundwork on Thursday. I suggest Stirling; that you try to delay the opening by a couple of weeks. Here's your copy of the plans and I'll take one around to the builder's shortly. You can contact the fencing company and give them the go ahead; they've given a completion date of three weeks time.'

'I will attempt to delay the opening, thanks for your help. When will we see you again?' asked Stirling.

'We'll call in regularly; I need to arrange for the security cameras and electrics to be installed. In the meantime, if you need us, call us. Okay Andi, let's go to the builders.'

A short journey later, they pulled up outside the builder's yard. Flats grabbed the plans from the back seat, 'Sorry boy, you'd better stay here.'

They went into the main office. 'I'm Mr. Magull and this is my daughter Andrea, is Mr. Hutchins in?'

'That's me,' said a man sat at a desk in one corner. 'You met my partner Mr. Grant last week, please, come and take a seat.'

'Was it you that I spoke to just now on the phone?'

'Yes it was; I believe you have some plans for me to look at.'

Flats handed them over and Mr. Hutchins unfurled the roll of paper. He used a stapler and hole punch to stop it rolling up again and stared at the plans. 'It's pretty much what we were expecting; we'll need to know very soon if you want us to build it.'

'If you can build this and keep within a hundred pounds of your quote, I can confirm that the job is yours.'

Mr. Hutchins held out his hand, 'We have a deal Mr. Magull; my men will be there on Thursday.'

The two of them shook hands before Flats and Andrea said goodbye and left.

'This is turning into a very busy day; where next pops, the station?'

'Yes cheeky, we still have a horse to find.

Chapter Nine

At the station; Isla was in the incident room with a few of her colleagues. 'How is it going?' enquired Flats.

'We are still hard at it but have managed to uncover some interesting information.'

Flats noticed a few folders lying on a table. 'Are these for me?'

'Yes but they're not quite complete,' informed WPC Knott, 'We have a little more to do. One of them contains a list of racing stables and stud farms near Cheltenham that we have found so far. There's another with information on both Lynch and Kelly which we believe is complete. They appear to be the most legitimate and solvent of the group.'

'Excellent work; by the way Isla, where's Nick?'

'Right here Flats,' Nick announced as he entered the room. 'I've been working with Hoskins compiling the list of stables, and we have a couple more to add to the list. I hope you don't mind me asking, but why concentrate your search relatively close to the race course itself?'

'Well according to the Chief Inspector in Cheltenham, they haven't seen a car towing a horse trailer on the roads or had reports of one. Therefore it makes sense that Sir Basil wasn't transported any great distance. We have to assume that he was taken up to thirty minutes before the alarm was raised, add to that the time it took for the police to arrive and put out the alert, at best, the vehicle could only have had an hour and a half, or so, to find a place to hide the horse. You certainly wouldn't be driving that fast with such a precious cargo. Therefore, I predict that they couldn't have gone more than fifty miles away, if that.'

'That makes sense; I understand your logic, thank you.'

'How many places have you found so far?'

'To be honest, I haven't counted but it can't be more than ten, the details are in this folder.'

Flats took the folder and sat down to study the contents with Andrea at his side. 'Now you told me that to catch a criminal, I need to think like one; but my first thought is whether there is a connection between the group and any of the stables. There are two places that stand out for me; and they are these two,' said Andrea showing the relevant documents.

'Interesting choices, so explain your reasoning to me.'

'Both of them have riding schools attached to them, and who ever heard of a top race horse being kept at one? I think it would be a perfect cover.'

'Those observations make very good sense, and of course, they would most likely have a trailer box as opposed to a Lorry type horsebox. Well done, now I need to phone Kenny; maybe he will know something about these two stables. Isla, is there a spare telephone that I can use?'

She pointed to a desk, 'Will that one be okay?'

Flats nodded and walked over to the desk. He picked up the phone and dialled. 'Hello Ken, it's Flats ….. Not bad thanks, I have some questions regarding a couple of stables, one is near Bath and the other in Congresbury ….. That's right; does the Shamrock Group have any connections with either of them? ….. I would be grateful. I will be here at the station on extension 275. Okay, speak to you soon.'

'Was he any help?' asked Andrea.

'Kenny's knows the stables and is aware of the trainers, although he doesn't know them personally. As far as he's aware, there is no connection with the group but he will make some enquiries and get back to me.'

Nick approached Flats; 'We have some financial background on all of them now. Messrs Lynch and Kelly are very well off with extremely healthy bank balances. Whelan and O'Donnell are also financially sound but not so well off as the first two. It seems that Finnegan and Nolan are the ones that are struggling, but why kidnap your own horse?'

'The most obvious reason is for insurance purposes and in light of what we know, I think they are desperate and we all know that desperate people do desperate things.' A phone rang, 'Flats, that's the one you used,' said Isla.

He walked over to the table and answered it. 'Hi Ken, what have you got? ..... I see ..... Tell him to call me at home later; you've got my number, bye for now.'

All eyes were on Flats, 'Kenny can't help, but Willie Wynne knows the jockeys at both stables and will talk to them and see if they can shed some light. As for me, I can't do anything more today so I will bid you all good evening.'

Andrea drove them back to the cottage. 'You know what, as there is still a bit of daylight left, I think I'll start erecting the new fencing around the hen house.'

'That's a good idea, I will help you then hopefully we can get our chickens a bit sooner. Can we have four this time?'

'I suppose so, one more won't make much difference, the coop is big enough, and there are three of us who enjoy the eggs,' he said with a smile. For the next hour they worked on the surrounding fence. 'There, that's done, all we need to do now is reinforce the bottom of the door and we are ready for our new brood.' declared Flats.

The two of them were just sitting down to eat when the phone rang. 'Typical, who can it be at this hour?' Flats went to take the call and returned moments later smiling. 'I think we might have a firm lead; that was Willie Wynne and according to Ben, the jockey at Kemble stud farm near Bath, they have just taken in three new mares. He's promised to find out where they've come from and call Willie tomorrow.'

'I don't understand; why would you breed a top stallion with a few ordinary mares? How would that earn any money and solve their financial problems?'

75

'Hmm, that's a very good point and I don't know the answer, but maybe Reg does. I'll give him a call after we've eaten. You're getting good at detective work and your thought process has come on leaps and bounds.'

'I have been thinking about becoming a Pathologist, like Dicky; do you think he would take on an apprentice?' Just imagine the benefits to us for future cases.'

'Knowing the man as I do, I'm sure he would welcome it and take you on. Ask him next time we see him, now I must give Reg that call.'

After several minutes, Flats returned to the kitchen. 'That was very interesting, he certainly knows his stuff. According to Reg, the mares are used to excite a stallion and when he mounts one of them, they collect his sample in a separate tube. He also gets to impregnate the mares in the hope that one of them produces a top foal. When it's old enough they enter it into a race and can make good money should it win, especially from betting on it, as the horse in question would be offered at high odds. In simple terms, they are entering a ringer.'

'But if that's the case, they would have to wait years to gain any benefit. Surely they need the money now.'

'Another good point Andi, something tells me there's more to this than meets the eye. Let's hope this jockey called Ben, can shed some light. I need to call Chief Inspector Godwin tomorrow to see if he had any luck with the TV crew, as to whether they caught anything on camera. I would love to know who the gentleman was that took the horse from the ginger haired lad. My guess is that he's tied in with Finnegan and or Nolan.'

Isla arrived home and breezed into the cottage, 'hello you two, something smells nice.'

'Yours is in the oven keeping warm,' said Andrea.

At that moment, the phone rang again. 'If we get many more calls I'll need a secretary,' muttered Flats as he went to answer it. When he came back he was wearing a very puzzled look.

'That was Aidan Lynch, he's just offered to match whatever Kenny is paying us, providing we find Sir Basil alive and well. This could be quite lucrative, but it throws up another question or two.'

'If he is willing to offer a further reward, then it's highly unlikely that he would be involved in the abduction.

Can't we get a warrant to search Kemble Farm?'

'It's too early for that as we don't have any real proof, but it does give me an idea, we should send someone to visit the place.'

'I'll go,' offered Andrea immediately, 'I could pose as someone interested in riding lessons.'

'Not so fast young lady; if it does prove to be the place where Sir Basil is being kept, chances are you could run into either Finnegan or Nolan, and you are known to them. We need someone that they don't know, and I think I know who, but that will have to wait until tomorrow, come on Jeeves let's go for a walk.'

Chapter Ten

Flats rose early and went into his garden; everything was now springing in to life. By the time he returned to the cottage, Andrea was up and making a pot of tea. 'Where are we going first today?' she asked him.

'To the station, I need to speak to the Chief. Is Isla still in bed?'

'No, she's in the shower; I believe she's doing the late shift today. When are we going for our new chickens? I do so miss my boiled egg for breakfast.'

'We'll go later after we've been to the station.'

The phone rang; 'I'll get it,' said Andrea.

'She returned a few moments later, it's for you.'

Flats went to the phone. 'Hello? ….. Oh good morning Willie ….. Yes, oh really? …... I see ….. Thanks for the information, please be careful ….. I'll pop over tomorrow and well done.'

'Who was that ringing so early? I really should have asked.'

'That was Willie Wynne, according to Ben at Kemble Farm; there are two men he hasn't seen before who have visited several times during the last week. Supposedly one is said to be a vet and the other specializes in breeding and generics. The stable has four horses owned by a Deidre Finnegan and the trainer's wife is Dara Nolan's sister. Ben also reckons that he was offered a bribe to throw a race but not by one of the aforementioned. There is one stable that is out of bounds to all staff and he is certain there are two horses inside. It looks like we may have got lucky; my hunch is that Sir Basil was taken there. I must make a quick call, and then if you're ready, we can head to the station?'

When they arrived, Andrea noticed a familiar vehicle in the car park. 'That's Dicky's car, what's he doing here?'

'I asked him to meet us here; he's paramount to my plan, although he doesn't know that yet.'

Flats went straight to the Chief's office; 'Would you join us in the incident room please, I'm going to need some assistance from you, if you don't mind.'

'Do I take it from your intonation that you have an idea where our missing horse may be?'

'I'll explain everything in the room. Good morning Dicky, thanks for coming,' he said as he spotted his friend talking to D.I. Crookes.

'I told you that I will always help and your call this morning has me intrigued.'

Flats addressed the room. 'Firstly I want to thank you all for your efforts in this case, we now believe we may have discovered the whereabouts of Sir Basil. Thanks to a call to the stable jockey at Kemble Farm near Bath, it seems extremely likely that our missing horse is being kept there. Chief, could you liaise with Bath station to get a search warrant, and inform Chief Inspector Godwin, from Cheltenham, of my plan. Now Dicky, this is where I need your help; I want you to visit Kemble with WPC Knott, posing as an interested party wanting riding lessons for a niece or young relative. See if you can get them to give you a tour of the stables. None of our suspects know either of you so it should be a good cover. Oh, by the way, buy some Sherbet Lemons, apparently the horse loves them. Hopefully, by the time we arrive the warrant will have been issued. If you come out from the farm and give us the thumbs up that the horse is there, the police can do their bit.'

'I assume WPC Knott will need to change before we go? Her uniform would give the game away.'

Flats nodded, 'It's probably a good idea for the pair of you to get going now.'

WPC Knott was excited at the idea of being out in the field. 'We can corroborate our story on the way,' she informed Dicky.

'What do you want me to do?' asked Nick.

'Check with the Chief to see if he needs you here, if not, we could certainly use an extra pair of hands. I'm sure the Bath force will be grateful too.'

When the Chief came back, he informed Flats that all would be in place. Bath branch have said that there is a Little Chef diner about a mile from Kemble and suggest you all rendezvous there. I've told Nick to take Hoskins; they've just left for him to get changed.'

'Andi, I think it's time that we left too,' said Flats.

'What about Dicky and Lynne, you know, WPC Knott? They've already left, how will they know where to meet the rest of us once they leave the farm?'

'Very good point Andrea, you leave it to me Flats, we'll think of something, now go,' said the Chief.

About an hour later, Flats and Andrea drove into the Little Chef car park. There were several unmarked cars but one had a blue light on the roof. He recognized the figure of Sergeant Best who was talking to another man. 'Good morning Sergeant, is everything in place?'

'Ah Mr. Magull, this is Sergeant Williams from Bath branch. The Chief Inspectors are inside supping tea. All the cars along this row belong to one or the other of the forces present. We also have a couple of motorbikes around the back; it was decided to keep them out of sight.'

'Who's the young lady?' enquired Sergeant Williams, 'is she plain clothes as well?'

'Oh no, that's my daughter Andrea and our dog Jeeves. She's just going to give him a short walk. Now if you would excuse me, I would like to get acquainted with the other members inside.'

As he entered the café, he was beckoned to one table.

'This is the gentleman that I told you about; Flats, meet Chief Inspector Curran from Bath.'

'Pleased to meet you, Chief Inspector Godwin here has filled me in on your joint investigation. I understand that a friend of yours will be going to the farm with a WPC. Can he be relied upon?'

'Dicky Martin is a pathologist with whom I've worked with on numerous occasions, trust me, he knows exactly what to do, and the WPC is very tenacious.' He looked at his watch; I expect them to be at the farm by now. Excuse me gents, I need to get a couple of coffees.'

~~~~

Dicky drove up the short track to the riding stable and as he parked, a woman wearing Jodhpurs and riding boots approached them. 'Can I help you?'

'Hopefully; my name is Richard and this is my daughter Lynne; we are looking for a riding school for a six year old and you were highly recommended.'

'That's nice to know; I'm Rose and I actually run the school. Tell me, has the little girl ridden before?'

'No, but she is horse mad so I thought she would love to learn. Could we have a look around?' asked Lynne.

'Of course, let me give a tour of the place. You may not be aware but we are also a stud farm for race horses.'

'Really, Oh I would love to see some of those close up, I've only ever seen them on the television,' said Lynne.

'This is the tack room; we encourage our students to take care of their horse after a lesson. Just simple things like brushing them and making sure they have feed. Now let me show you our horses and ponies. We have eleven altogether, and as you can see here in the paddock, there are various sizes catering for all ages.'

After the tour of the school, Dicky politely reminded Rose about the race horses. She was happy to oblige and Lynne was so thrilled to be close to the muscular beasts.

'Tell me, what's in this other building?' he asked.

'That's part of our breeding program; we only have one horse at the moment.'

'Can we see it, if it's possible?' pushed Dicky, wondering whether Rose was aware of any dirty dealings going on.

'I suppose it won't hurt, but I should warn you, he's very

temperamental.' As she opened the top door of the stable, Dicky winked at Lynne. She stepped away; 'Why are these two stables empty.'

Rose moved towards her and explained that they were expecting some other horses for the breeding program. Meanwhile, Dicky took advantage of the distraction to dig into his pocket and pull out a Sherbet Lemon. The horse immediately came to the door to accept the treat. 'I think he likes me,' said Dicky stroking the horse's head.

'You must have a way with horses Richard,' complimented Rose.

Lynne joined him and reached to stroke its mane whilst studying the marks on its head.

Rose looked at her watch; 'we must move out of here now, the vet will be along shortly and he doesn't take kindly to visitors being in here.'

'That's fine; I think we have seen enough, don't you Lynne?'

'Yes dad, do you have a brochure or something with your number on please Rose?'

'Of course, I'll get you one on the way out.'

With a brochure in her hand, Lynne got into the car as

Dicky started the engine; 'Thank you, we will be in touch,' she said ironically.

As he drove back down the track his thoughts turned to where Flats and the police would be. 'All we have to do now is find Flats and the team and I have no idea which way to go.'

At the end of the track, he paused. Opposite, was a motorcyclist sitting on his bike smoking a cigarette. He looked at Dicky and made a short gesture pointing up the road. 'I guess that's our clue,' he said as he turned out of the track. Moments later the motorbike flashed past and then slowed. When they reached the Little Chef, he indicated and pulled in. Dicky noticed Andrea's car and smiled, 'They're here.'

Flats greeted his friend; 'How did it go?'

'Like clockwork, the old Dicky Martin charm worked its magic, admirably aided by Lynne here. Sir Basil is there, we are certain. I gave him a Sherbet Lemon, according to your instructions, which he greedily accepted. The markings on his face are different but Lynne assures me that someone has used a type of hair colouring, or dye, to cover the white blaze.'

'If you look close you can see a rectangular patch covering where his white patch should be. It's very subtle but different,' informed Lynne.

After a tactical briefing, the police left to go and raid the farm.

'You should go Nick, you're representing Yeovil station,' said Flats.

'Why aren't we going?' asked Andrea.

'They have more than enough bodies, and, from what Dicky told me, there are only a few people at the farm. We'd only be in the way so let's go home, you can drive. Thanks for your help Dicky, fancy a pint later?'

'Good idea, I'll see you there about eight. I need to drop Lynne back at the station and run a couple of errands first.'

'Are we still getting our chickens today?'

'In all the excitement, I'd forgotten about them; yes we can do that on the way home.'

Chapter Eleven

It was late in the evening by the time Isla returned from work. 'I'm disappointed that I missed all the fun but they've found what they believe to be the horse and made several arrests. A vet was called to check over the horse and the stable's jockey asked to be taken in too, something to do with bribery, I'll know more tomorrow.'

'They'll need a hairdresser as well to remove the dye from that poor horse,' quipped Andrea.

'I understand that you're off to the pub soon, give me ten minutes to shower and change and I'll join you. Oh Knotty's coming too; I think she's taken a shine to Dicky; apparently she enjoyed being his 'daughter' for the day.'

As Isla disappeared up the stairs, Flats asked Andrea if WPC Knott was single.

'Yes, I believe so, but she does have a little girl. You're not thinking about her and Dicky getting together are you? There's such a big age gap.'

'Stranger things have happened, and he can be quite a charmer at times.'

There was a celebratory atmosphere at the pub and many from the station had decided to join the group. Flats collared Nick, 'I gather the raid was a success.'

'To a degree, yes, but we were discussing the situation; that is myself, the two Chief's from Bath and Cheltenham and a couple of Sergeants. We're not sure if we can charge someone for kidnapping their own horse, assuming we can pin that on the Shamrock Group. What really needs investigating now is whether it's related to race fixing and illegal artificial insemination. Apparently the Jockey Club are interested in how the police proceed with the case. Ben Collis is giving information regarding the bung he was offered to throw a couple of races. The forensic team is checking the horse trailer at Kemble Farm for finger prints, to see if they match those found on the stolen horsebox. I'll keep you posted.'

~~~~

The following morning, Flats was woken by the smell of fresh coffee. When he came downstairs, Isla was sat at the kitchen table. 'Have you seen Jeeves?'

'He's outside with Andi attending to your new chickens; those two are as thick as thieves. What are you doing today?'

'Do you know, I'm not sure, but as it's a nice day, I

think I should blow the cobwebs out of Vinnie. In fact, now I come to think of it, that sounds like a good idea.' Flats went outside to the chicken house. 'Couldn't you sleep?'

'I thought that you deserved a lie in; Jeeves and I had a nice long walk. Sadly, we don't have any eggs today.'

'Oh, I'm glad you mentioned that, give me minute.' He then went into the garden shed and, after a couple of minutes, re-emerged wearing a broad grin. 'I found them; these are ceramic eggs, we need to put them in the nesting boxes. It gives the chickens an idea where to lay their eggs; otherwise you'll find them on the floor.'

'Is that the reason why we have no eggs?'

'No, we bought these birds as POL which stands for 'point of lay'. It means they are due to start laying eggs any day now, just be patient. By the way, I was thinking of taking Vinnie out soon, if you're interested.'

'Yes please, it will give me a chance to wear my new biker's gear. What will you do with Jeeves?'

'This is one of the few times that he'll have to stay indoors, he will hate it but it won't be for long.'

Isla left for work as Flats and Andrea sat down to have a quick cup of tea before heading off. The telephone rang

so Flats answered it. 'Hello Kenny ….. You what? …..
Tell him we will be there.' Flats sat back down.

'That was Kenny; Aiden Lynch is going to his stable
later and would like to see us, so that's decided where
we're going for our ride.'

Just before they got on the motorbike, Flats explained to
Andrea what she needed to do. 'When we come to a
bend, you must lean into it, so if the bend is to the left,
you lean to the left and vice versa for right bends. Try
not to stay upright, lean with the bike; I'm sure you'll
soon the hang of it.'

The engine roared into life and Flats showed Andrea
how to get on. 'There's a bar behind you to hold onto,
are you ready?' He could see her nod in his mirror and
with a clunk to select first gear, they were off. The first
bend they came to, Andrea felt a little nervous but did
exactly as she was instructed. It was an exhilarating
experience for her and she enjoyed the feeling.
Eventually they arrived at Kenny's stables. 'That was
amazing, I want my own motorbike now,' gushed
Andrea.

Flats noticed Kenny talking to a man dressed smartly in
a suit. 'Ah Flats, glad you could make it, this is Aidan
Lynch come and say hello.'

'Pleased to meet you Mr. Lynch, this is my daughter Andrea.'

Aidan acknowledged her, then reached into his pocket and took out an envelope. 'This is what I promised you; thank you for finding our horse. Tell me, do you have any idea who took him?'

Flats took a deep breath; 'I hate to tell you, but there is strong evidence to suggest that at least a couple of your fellow group members were responsible, or at least had some involvement. The police are deciding how to progress with the evidence they have.'

'Would you mind telling me who you suspect?'

'Mr. Finnegan and Mr. Nolan,' replied Andrea.

There was a brief uncomfortable silence. 'I need to call my partner Sean; is there a phone handy please Ken?'

'Sure, you can use the one in the office over there, be my guest.'

'He didn't look too happy,' observed Andrea.

'I think we can probably rule him out of any investigation relating to the abduction,' said Flats.

As they waited for Aidan to return, Kenny gave Flats a

cheque. 'I hope that's okay for you.' Flats glanced at the details, thanked him and put it safely away.

When Aidan came back he was looking a little flustered. 'Sean is fuming; we have made the decision to buy the other member's shares in Sir Basil. Kenny; We want that horse back in your stable as soon as possible, will you take care of it?'

'I'll get in touch with the relevant police force to establish when the horse can be released,' offered Flats.

'Will you be pressing charges against those involved?' enquired Kenny.

'No, that's not the Irish way; we will handle this amongst our own. I must leave now; I have much to take care of. I'll see you again soon Kenny; as for you Flats, and your delightful daughter, if you're ever near one of our restaurants, drop in, it'll be on the house.'

As Aidan drove off, Kenny turned to his friend; 'It looks like you've just made a friend for life and I've got my star stallion back, well soon anyway.'

'It looks that way, now we should be going but we'll drop in again soon.' He started the engine, and with Andrea comfortably seated, they rode away.

When they arrived at the police station, Andrea was

puzzled; 'Why are we here?'

'I want to have a quick chat with Nick and phone calls made from here are free,' he replied with a wink.

'Perhaps you will allow me to make some of the calls.'

Inside the station; Flats said hello to Hoskins before enquiring if Nick was in. 'You'll find him loitering somewhere twiddling his thumbs. Who's the biker chick?' he teased.

Andrea gave him a friendly slap as she passed; 'Is that the best you can come up with Sarge?'

Nick was surprised to see them. 'What brings you here?'

'I need some numbers please; let me see, Bath station and Kemble Farm will do for starters.'

'You know who the best person to ask is, she's at her usual desk. If you don't mind me asking, why do you need them?'

'Just tidying things up before I finish with the case.'

Flats and Andrea went to WPC Knott's desk and asked for the relevant numbers. She found them with her usual efficiency and wrote them on a piece of paper. After thanking her, Flats tore the paper into two pieces and gave one to Andrea. 'There you go, give them a call and ask if the horse is still there, who's taking care of it and whether the horse trailer is still there. I'll call Bath station and see what they have to say.'

They were directed to a couple of spare phones. After making their calls they returned to WPC Knott's desk. Isla had also entered the office and was surprised to see her friends there.

'Come on then Flats, we're dying to know what this is all about,' said Nick.

'One moment; Andi, what did you find out from Kemble?'

'Sir Basil is still there and being cared for by Ben Collis and an assistant of the riding school. They are struggling to cope with all the horses due to the lack of staff ….. Oh, and the trailer is still there in the yard.'

Flats looked at the phone on the desk; 'May I?' Lynne nodded so he picked up the phone and dialled. 'Hello Ken, it's Flats here, I've spoken to the Chief Inspector at Bath and he informs me that you can collect Sir Basil whenever you're ready ….. Really? That's good, I'm sure they will be very relieved ….. Okay my friend, bye for now.'

Flats looked at the faces of the others all waiting in expectation. 'I bet you're all wondering what that was all about,' he teased. 'Bath police have said that they are happy to let Sir Basil be removed. Aidan Lynch and Sean Kelly have negotiated a deal to buy out the other member's stakes in him. They also now own the three mares that were taken to Kemble Farm. Kenny is sending his horsebox to collect all four horses and will train them at his place. The trailer has been impounded, albeit left in situ on the farm. The Shamrock Group is no more and the Jockey Club are investigating Messrs Finnegan and Nolan for certain irregularities pertaining to betting and possible race fixing. It would appear that the statement Ben Collis made implicates both of them in this matter. He gave a very good detailed description of the two men that have been visiting the farm over the last week or so, one of them matches the description of the person who took the horse from our ginger haired lad at Cheltenham. There you have it, a good job and a happy conclusion. Now we need to head home, poor Jeeves will be climbing the walls. Oh, if any of you are up for it, Andi and I are in the chair for the drinks tonight.'

On the way out of the station, Flats extended the invitation to Hoskins and the Chief.

Chapter Twelve

That evening everyone was in a celebratory mood. Flats was sat talking to Dicky with Andrea, as usual, by his side, whilst WPC Knott was sitting very close to Dicky, something that hadn't gone unnoticed by several of the revellers. Andrea mentioned her ride as a pillion passenger and how much she'd enjoyed it.

'My dear girl; if you are going to sit behind this lunatic, make sure it's not at night on dark country roads,' said Dicky with an artful grin.

'Oh come on, leave it out; that was years ago, no one's interested in hearing about it.'

By now, everyone was looking at Dicky. 'I think you should let us be the judges of that, pray tell,' insisted Isla.

'Many years ago, when we were hell raising teenagers, most of our friends had motorbikes. Speedy here had an AJS Silver Streak, which in its day was quick, much faster than the bikes most of us had. One particular night, we left the pub deciding to head for the beach. Flats was the last out and told us to get going as he would catch us up. He was quite cocky in those days, but we all loved him for it. I have to admit that he was the best rider out of all of us. Well we shot off into the night; I think you should tell the rest of this story Flats.'

'Okay, okay; what I should mention is that war had broken out so lighting was extremely minimal. Anyway, I raced after Dicky and the rest of them. Eventually I caught sight of a tail light, and as he had the slowest machine, assumed it was Dicky. For some inexplicable reason to me now, I switched off my headlights so he wouldn't know that I was coming. There was a left hand bend ahead so I gave it everything on the throttle. As we came off the bend, I decided that I would squeeze up his inside to give him a scare.' He paused for a moment as though he was re-counting that night. 'Just as I caught him and was about to race up his inside, I realised that it wasn't Dicky at all but by then it was too late. I ended up clattering my AJS into the back of a bus and I landed on the stairs. In those days you got on at the back of the bus which is where the stairs to the top deck were. Because of the blackout in those days, the bus had no interior lights and just the offside rear light.'

Everyone began to laugh at Flats' misfortune.

'It's alright for you lot, I felt a right idiot; my bike was a mess ….. And I had a broken wrist to boot. The bus driver was none too happy either and gave me an earful. What made it even worse was that Dicky, and the others, had stopped for a cigarette to wait for me. When I didn't arrive, they came back to look for me, and you can imagine the stick I took from them.'

'It did slow you down for a while,' teased Dicky.

'That's an understatement, do you know that I had to rely on him to take me everywhere while my precious AJS was being repaired. His bike was so slow that an 80 year old on a pushbike rode passed us ….. And that was going uphill.'

'You could have walked you know,' countered Dicky.

'What! And embarrass you further by getting there before you?'

The banter between the two friends was infectious and made the whole pub laugh. Finally the Landlord called time and, after emptying their glasses, everyone went home.

~~~~

It was late in the morning when the phone rang. 'Hello Larry ….. WHAT! ….. Yes of course ….. I'll leave immediately ….. Okay, will do.'

'That sounded serious, what's happened?'

'Ben Collis was found hanged this morning in one of the stables at Kemble Farm. Larry wants to see me, well actually both of us, right away. I just need to ring Dicky and then we should go immediately to find out why we're needed.'

The station was a hive of activity. 'It's a rum business Flats,' said Hoskins as they entered the building. The Chief was waiting for them and ushered them into the incident room.

'What's all this about and why do you need us?'

'Chief Inspector Curran phoned me first thing to inform me of the news. He's not happy with what they've found and he can't get hold of his pathologist. I offered to ask Dicky for his services and he would also like you to attend. They found a suicide note from Ben, but in light of the information he gave, Curran suspects foul play. Would you be willing to assist the Bath branch? You will, of course, be paid for your services.'

'Yes of course, we can leave as soon as Dicky arrives. Can I make a request for Nick to come along as he is familiar with everything we know so far?'

'He's all yours, between you and me; I think he was

hoping you would ask. I understand that representatives of the Jockey Club will meet you there too, they are also hoping for your assistance.'

Dicky came hurriedly into the room; 'Flats said that I was needed, what can I do.'

After receiving a quick summary of events, he volunteered to drive his car but the Chief said that they should go in one of the high performance squad cars. 'You may find the blue lights come in helpful at some point. Give me a minute.' He went to the front desk and spoke to Sergeant Hoskins. 'Okay gents, and Andrea of course, your transport will be out front in a couple of minutes; good luck.'

Outside the station, Sergeant Hoskins was waiting in one of the forces' newest acquisitions.

'Does the Chief know you've taken this vehicle?' questioned Nick.

'It was his idea, this Range Rover is perfect for five adults, and there's plenty of room for Jeeves in the back. Did you see the light on the roof?'

'My dear boy, that bulbous thing spoils the look of such a nice vehicle,' answered Dicky sarcastically.

An hour later, Hoskins drove the vehicle up the track to

Kemble Farm. There were many vehicles parked already in situ. As they alighted from the car, a man hurried across to them.

'Mr. Magull, so glad you made it, thanks for coming.'

'Chief Inspector Curran, this is Dicky Martin, our pathologist, Inspector Nick Crookes, Sergeant Hoskins, and you know my daughter. Would you like to bring us up to speed?'

'We were called this morning by Rose, the lady who runs the riding school, she found our victim hanging from one of the beams in the race horse stable. There was a suicide note on the floor but my instincts tell me that something isn't right. Mr. Martin, would you like to check out the crime scene so that we can cut down the victim and release his body?'

'Of course Chief, let me get my bag.'

They headed for the stables; 'this may be an unpleasant sight Andi, are you sure you're up to it?' asked Flats.

'If I want to study pathology then I have to get used to seeing these things,' she replied.

'Did I hear you say you want to study pathology Andi? I trust you will come to me to learn.'

'Yes, I've been meaning to ask you for your help, I'm very keen to learn.'

'Well then my dear girl, there is no time like the present.' He held out his hand which she took. 'This is not only Flats' daughter, but my darling goddaughter too Chief,' he declared proudly.

Inside the stable, Dicky looked at the limp body hanging from the beam. 'We need to be quick but also thorough; I don't want that body there any longer than necessary. First thing, photographs, take plenty and from all angles.'

They watched as Dicky took out his camera and began snapping away. 'Now then Andi, observations, study the scene for clues as to how this happened. The first noticeable oddity is the distance from his feet to the ground. He would have needed a ladder to get that high but there isn't one anywhere in sight. So before we cut him down, we need to measure the distance from his feet to the ground.' As soon as it was done, Dicky turned to the Chief, 'Okay, he can be taken down now.'

'One moment Dicky, look at this,' said Andrea, 'check the seat of his trousers, it's covered in hairs.'

'Well spotted young lady, that maybe a clue.'

Flats had put on a pair of gloves and was studying the suicide note. 'Chief; who found this first?'

'I believe it was Rose.'

'Has anyone else handled it without wearing gloves?'

'As far as I know, just one of my officers.'

'In that case, I need to see both of them and take their finger prints,' informed Dicky.

After finding a ladder, the body was carefully lowered to the ground. Dicky took several more photographs and then ordered that the body be taken to the morgue. 'Leave the rope in place please, now then Andi, let's get these finger prints taken ….. Oh, and can you take these tweezers and this bag to retrieve a few of the hairs from the deceased's trousers ….. or would you rather I do it?'

'No, I'm fine, I have to start somewhere,' she said bravely.

Chapter Thirteen

Flats was having a good look around the stable and yet again found a cigar butt. He carefully picked it up and put it into an evidence bag which Nick gave him.

'Why is there a horse walking around quite freely?' asked Flats.

'Would you like me to get her?' offered Hoskins.

'Yes please, and then bring her into the stable if you don't mind.'

'How do you know it's a 'her'? Queried Nick.

'Take a close look sir and you will notice, the absence of any 'dangly' bits,' he replied with a chuckle.

Hoskins then led the horse into the stable and, as requested by Flats, positioned the mare under the beam from which Ben was found hanging.

'What do you think gentlemen, this horse is about the right size and bearing in mind the hairs on poor Ben's trousers, I would suggest that this horse was used. He could have sat on her and then made her walk on. But why would he commit suicide? And then there's this alleged note.'

I'm sorry for making false accusations to the police. I feel so ashamed, it's best this way.

'I don't buy it Flats, that don't seem right,' said Hoskins.

'That's my thoughts exactly; I need to speak to Dicky.'

They caught up with him in the office; Dicky looked up at Flats; 'something does not feel right my friend, Rose here was telling us that Ben appeared in good spirits yesterday. Apart from the extra work he had thrust upon him, he seemed happy.'

'Well we found a loose horse wandering around, and it's my assumption that Ben was on this particular horse prior to his demise. You'll find the animal tethered inside the stable block,' Flats informed him.

'Come on Andi my dear, we need to get some hair samples from this horse, be back in a minute folks.'

Flats turned to Rose; 'What did you make of this suicide note? I was told that you found it.'

'Yes, that's right, but it's not Ben's handwriting. I don't wish to speak ill of the dead, but he wrote like a little child. He was brilliant with horses and a superb jockey but his writing wasn't very good. Hold on a minute and I'll see if I can find a sample of his handwriting.'

Rose rifled through some drawers in a filing cabinet and pulled out a folder. She opened it and showed those present; 'Do you see what I mean?'

'That's totally different to the note,' observed Nick.

'Precisely, thank you for your help Rose. Will you be able to cope with the horses on your own?'

'Yes, the riding school has been closed until further notice; and I've turned the ponies and horses out into paddocks. I'm expecting Mr. Race's horsebox any minute to collect Sir Basil and three of the mares. Another owner, who has some horses here, will be collecting them tomorrow. That will make it a bit easier for me to keep the place ticking over.'

'Very good; Chief, once Dicky has finished, we should gather everyone together to go over what we know and to formulate a plan as to how we should proceed.'

'That's an excellent suggestion Mr. Magull, thank you for all your help today.'

They all gathered on the car park where Dicky was the first to speak. 'I need to get to the morgue to do an autopsy and then check the note for prints.'

'I'll have one of my men take you and your assistant there now,' said the Chief. 'What's your next move Flats.'

'Well I was led to believe that representatives of the Jockey Club were going to be here, so I will hang on a bit longer and then join up with Dicky at the morgue.'

Right on cue, a car drove up the track, and two men got out; 'Which one of you is Mr. Magull?'

'That's me and who are you?'

'John Benson and Rob Hedges, we're from the Jockey Club,' answered one of the men. 'We were made aware of allegations made by Ben Collis and want to follow it up with your assistance please.'

'Certainly gentlemen, would you be able to speak with the television company to ascertain if they have any footage of the stables during that day? I'm interested in the man who led Sir Basil away from them. We do have a good description and we have a strong inclination that the same person has been here within the last week. Chief, can I get a copy of Ben's statement?'

'I'll have one faxed to Yeovil station. We at Bath are running checks on the Shamrock Group members.'

'So are we,' said Nick, 'in fact, ours are almost complete. I presume you are aware that the group has been disbanded.'

'No I wasn't, in that case, would you mind liaising with D.I. Phelps, we can then see if either of us has missed anything?' requested the Chief.

'I think he means what they have missed,' whispered Hoskins to Nick, who smiled knowingly at the comment.

A horsebox came rattling up the track and Flats recognised one of the men. 'Hello Kenny, I guess you've come to collect the horses.'

'Oh yes, and we can't wait to get Sir Basil back to his stable, I even came armed with Sherbet Lemons.'

Rose came and offered to help load the horses. Flats turned his attention to Messrs Benson and Hedges from the Jockey Club.

'Now then gents, exactly what do you want me to do?'

'We were hoping to use, and of course remunerate you, in respect of your expertise to expose those who are trying to bring our sport into disrepute. I think you are aware that the favourite in the first race was drugged, hence his poor showing.'

'Yes, I had heard; it is my opinion that the gentleman I want to identify, who has at least one accomplice, is heavily involved. I also suspect at least two members, of the now defunct Shamrock Group, are also complicit in some way or another.'

One of the men produced a card, 'Here's our number; we will give you whatever support and help that we can. You can also send us your bill to the address on the card. Please tread carefully; we suspect that there are some shady characters involved who won't take too kindly to being exposed.'

'Gentlemen, it won't be the first time that I've had dealings with persons of dubious intent, but thank you for your concern. Now if you'll excuse me, I'd like to have a last look around this place. I'll be in touch in due course. Good day to you.'

'What are we looking for?' asked Nick.

'Anything, everything, I want another look at the crime scene and the area around it. It will be interesting to see the autopsy report, hopefully that will shed some light. Excuse me, Chief Inspector Curran, would you have the stable cordoned off please? And try to limit the number of people who enter it to essential forensic team members only.'

'Certainly, is there anywhere else to be cordoned off?'

'Ideally I would like the whole farm off limits except for Rose who has to look after a number of animals.'

'Leave it to me; that can be arranged.'

Flats went back to the stable with Nick and Hoskins to where Ben was found hanging. He looked up at the beam and then down at the ground. 'The only way the rope could have been secured around that beam is with a ladder, probably the same one that was used to cut down Ben's body. So if we're supposed to believe it was suicide, he would have had to secure the rope himself before putting the ladder away, and with his hands tied.'

'I don't mean to be impertinent or facetious Flats, but that sounds a bit farfetched to me.'

'Exactly Hoskins, this was definitely murder, I think we should go to the morgue to see how Dicky is faring.'

On the way to the car, Flats spoke to Rose; 'Do not let anyone take anything from the farm, except for the pre-arranged removal of horses; the whole area is now a crime scene. If you have any problems, call the police immediately.' They then informed the Chief that they were all leaving, and after a brief discussion, plus getting directions to the morgue, they went on their way.'

Chapter Fourteen

As they attempted to enter the morgue, a gentleman at the door refused to allow them in.

Flats gave him an icy stare. 'May I ask who you are and what your position is here?'

'My name is not important but I am the Diener and I say who is permitted entry.'

'We are here to see my friend Mr. Richard Martin who is here with, um, his assistant. Please tell him that Flats is here and he will confirm it.'

'Okay, you may enter; he did tell me to expect you.'

Flats thanked him as he brushed past. Dicky and Andrea were sat at a desk busily writing. As they approached, he looked up at them through wistful eyes. 'This was a particularly nasty murder that shows a complete disregard for human life. You have got to catch these perpetrators, but for goodness sake Flats, be extremely careful.'

His words had a chilling effect on all present. 'Okay, you're the second person to warn me. Pray tell me what you've discovered.'

Dicky cleared his throat and spoke in a sombre voice; 'Ben was already dead, or at least unconscious, before he was hanged. When we removed the rope from around his neck, I noticed the area from his chin to his throat had rope burns. Andrea and I pondered this for a while and came to the conclusion that Ben was placed on the horse and due to being unconscious, he would have slumped forward onto his chest.'

'Can you explain why you believe that he was unconscious?'

'I was coming to that, but as you ask; there is a needle mark below his right ear. We found a high dosage of the horse tranquilizer Xylazine in his blood; enough to knock him out, that's for sure. The rope was put around his neck and the body hoisted upright. Now please excuse my choice of words, but as the body would now be dead weight, it most probably took two men to get him bolt upright.' Dicky then paused.

'We believe that Ben was caught off guard,' added Andrea. 'There were no signs of a struggle, and after re-enacting what we think happened, our conclusion is that whoever administered the drug was left handed and came at him from behind, catching him unaware.'

'Sorry Flats, for some reason, this death got to me, the poor boy was about Andi's age and he had so much to live for. His death was caused by strangulation, such a waste of a life. At least he was unconscious which means he wouldn't have suffered.'

'How much longer will you need to conclude your report?' asked Flats.

'We are just about done; maybe another five minutes and we will be ready to leave.'

'What's our next move Flats?' queried Nick.

'Bath police station, I'm not waiting for them to fax Ben's statement through, I want a copy; NOW!'

As soon as Dicky was ready, they all left and headed to Bath station. Flats spoke to the Chief Inspector and was told that the statement from Ben Collis would be faxed through to Yeovil as previously mentioned.

'I guess that I will have to fax my copy of the autopsy by the same means when we return to Yeovil,' said Dicky.

'If you have the report then I'll take it from you now.'

'No Chief, it doesn't work that way, if you want my report now, then you have to give us the statement in return. 'Quid pro quo' I believe.'

For a moment the Chief paused; 'Wait here.'

'Make that two copies please,' demanded Flats.

He came back clutching a file and reluctantly handed it over. Flats took a quick look and nodded to Dicky who then passed a document to the Chief. 'There you are, that's my report,' he said.

Without another word, Flats and his team left the building. 'What an obnoxious man,' said Andrea.

'He's probably not thrilled with the idea of another force operating on his patch,' replied Hoskins, 'He'll want to solve this crime himself; but my money is on our man Flats to beat him to it.'

Andrea smiled and nodded in agreement.

Eventually they arrived at the Yeovil station where the Chief was eager for an update. 'The Commissioner is taking an interest in this investigation because there are three forces involved, and he is hoping to be put in over all control of it.'

'Well there's not much more that we can do today, I suggest we all come at it fresh in the morning.' Dicky informed him that he would stay a little longer to finish up some paperwork before going home. Flats nodded and left clutching a copy of Ben's statement.

Back at the cottage, Andrea asked to have a look at the statement. 'Be my guest, I'm going to give Jeeves some exercise in the field at the back; now where did we put his ball?'

'I can read this later; I'd rather be with you two.'

When Isla came home she could hear squeals of laughter and plenty of barking. Being curious, she walked up through the garden in the direction of the sounds. 'You lot look as though you're having fun.' Before they could answer, she climbed the stile to join them.

'That's enough,' puffed Flats, 'I need a drink.'

As soon as they were indoors, Andrea put the kettle on. 'I'll make a pot of tea and feed Jeeves.'

After getting changed, Isla entered the lounge; 'I nearly forgot, the Commissioner would like to see you at the station in the morning. Don't ask me why because he didn't say. Now Andi, tell me about your day as a budding pathologist.'

Flats left the girls chatting and went into the kitchen; he sat at the table and began to study Ben's Statement.

After reading it several times he began to feel tired, so he bid goodnight to the young women and made his way upstairs.

~~~~

Early next morning he woke feeling refreshed and ready for the day ahead. The sun was shining as he went outside to the garden. Jeeves was in a mischievous mood and wanted to play. 'You have far too much energy for this time of day.' As he fed the chickens he noticed an egg in one of the nesting boxes. He carefully put it in his pocket and returned to the cottage. Isla was there and he showed her the egg.

'The first from our new brood, one of you can have a boiled egg for breakfast.'

'That will be me; I'll boil some water and make a pot of tea. By the way, what did you make of Ben's statement?'

'We have some clear suspects but no real evidence as yet. I want to find this so called vet and breeding expert;

they are certainly involved with the killing. This is going to be a challenge.'

'If it's any consolation, all of us at the station are behind you and ready to help.'

'Good morning you two,' greeted Andrea sleepily. 'When did we buy any eggs?'

'We didn't, it's the first from our new brood. Isla bagged it; you'll have to wait until tomorrow for another. Hopefully they will all be laying soon. I'm going to the station shortly; you can get a lift with Isla.'

Chapter Fifteen

When Flats arrived at the station, the desk clerk informed him that the Commissioner was in the Chief's office waiting for him. 'Ah Mr. Magull and his trusty companion, thank you for coming, take a seat.'

'Thank you commissioner, what can I do for you?'

'It's this sad business with the jockey and his allegations. I have been tasked with overseeing the three forces involved in the investigation. I know that the Jockey Club have hired you and I believe you are highly regarded by a couple of members of the now disbanded Shamrock Group. To that end, I am taking the unprecedented decision of asking you to head the enquiry. If you are willing to accept this responsibility; I will inform all concerned and you can select your own team. Inspector Crookes will be overseeing the daily running of this station so he won't be fully available. There are several new additions arriving for him to induct and allocate duties to. The Chief Inspector has expressed a desire to be involved, which I strongly support. Do you have any questions?'

'No commissioner, you have made yourself abundantly clear. I will be happy to take charge of this investigation and will begin immediately to assemble a team.'

He went to the incident room where he found Nick on his own. 'Sorry Flats, I would love to be fully involved but the commissioner has other plans for me.'

'Don't you worry, I'll make sure you're kept up to speed and given plenty of opportunity to assist when you can. Talking of which, I would like this room re-arranged and a couple more desks added.'

He then gave details of exactly what he wanted.

'Leave that to me, I'll grab a couple of spare men and take care of that now.'

Andrea and Isla came into the room; 'I'm getting this incident room ready; the commissioner has asked me to take charge of this investigation as he is overseeing the three forces. We have much to do; Andi would you look after Jeeves for me, I need to assemble my team and Isla, naturally, your one of them.'

Flats found WPC Knott in another room; 'no doubt you've heard what's happening, would you grab your things and report to the incident room?'

She didn't need asking twice and swiftly gathered up her paperwork and things just as the Sergeant poked his head around the door.

'Ah Hoskins, I wondered when you were going to turn up, would you please join us in the incident room.'

'Certainly, I'd be delighted to.'

Flats addressed his team and gave them each different responsibilities. 'Hoskins, would you please speak to the Jockey Club and ask if they've had any luck with the TV Company? If they have any footage, request a copy then circulate the pictures to try to put a name to the face. Isla; can you arrange for an artist to sketch photo fits of the two men seen at Kemble Farm? Lynne; your main task is collect and collate the information as it comes in from the other forces and assist wherever it's needed. If any of you need additional help, you have permission to bring available bodies into the team. Andi, we need to start a suspect and information board, In the meantime, I have a couple of calls to make.'

When he returned, everyone was very busy; 'I need to go to Kenny's yard,' he announced. Andi sprang to her feet and grabbed her bag and coat; meanwhile Flats gathered a few documents and put them in a folder. When he informed the Chief of his intentions, he asked if he could tag along. 'We can take my car if you like.'

'I hope you won't mind it getting covered in hair.'

'Of course not, I'll just put it in for a clean.'

Kenny was pleased as usual to see his friend. 'I'm not sure if you've met Chief Inspector Bottle.'

The men shook hands before Flats enquired if Willie was around. 'He's in the stallion's stable; do you wish to speak to him?'

'Yes please, I just want to ask him a few questions.'

They all walked to the stable where they found Willie assisting one of the stable lads.

Kenny called him over; 'Flats would like a word.'

'Sure thing, how can I help?'

'Ben Collis gave a statement accusing a few people of attempting to bribe him to throw races. Would you know anything about this and have you ever been approached?'

'Of course I've been offered bribes; and been pressurised to throw a race, but I tell those people where to go. I haven't had anyone approach me for a while; perhaps they know that I can't be bought. As for Ben; he was, and I don't mean to be harsh, a somewhat simple soul. I know he struggled with writing and his maths in general was poor, but he was a good person and very good jockey. He could remember all the horses that he ever rode and the position he finished. We were riding at Exeter last month and he said someone had threatened him if he didn't throw a race.'

'When you have been approached, was it by the same person on every occasion?'

'No, but there was one man who spoke to me a few times, I believe he was Irish.'

'Would you be able to give a full description of this person to a police artist?' asked the Chief.

'Yes, I think so. When would you like me to do this?'

Flats looked at Kenny; 'Can you spare him now? We could take him back to the station with us and bring him straight back afterwards.'

Kenny nodded; 'If it helps you to catch the killer, of course he can go with you, I'm sure we can mange for a few hours.'

'Okay, we'll be on our way,' said the Chief.

Flats thanked his friend; 'I'll bring him back personally when we're done. Then we can have a chin wag over a coffee, or tea.'

At the station, the Chief explained to Hoskins what he required; 'Can I leave Mr. Wynne in your capable hands? Let us know when he's finished.'

'Yes Chief; would you mind following me Willie.'

Flats went to the incident room and approached the desk where WPC Knott was sitting. 'Have you uncovered any more information?'

'We are just in the process of completing our files on the 'Shamrock Six' which is what we've named them. Cheltenham has called and it seems we may be in luck regarding the television cameras. The TV Company are screening their reels of film for a decent shot of our mystery man. Isla has updated the suspect board.'

'If you look Flats, we now have some photographs of the six. Taking into consideration your thoughts, Finnegan and Nolan are the most likely suspects, so they're in the middle. Spaces for Whelan and O'Donnell are one side and there are two spaces for the men seen at Kemble Farm on the other. Messrs Lynch and Kelly have been placed on the periphery. Although you don't think they're involved, I've included them until we have a conviction or two.'

'That's very good; what about Bath? Have they managed to get descriptions of the alleged vet and breeder from Rose or anyone else at Kemble Farm?' asked Flats.

'They're hoping to have artist impressions of them very soon and will fax them across,' Lynne informed him.

'Where would they do their gambling?' asked Andrea, 'I was wondering if anything shows up on their bank statements.'

'Already in hand, we are trawling though that information at the moment, but nothing in particular stands out,' replied Lynne.

A phone rang ….. 'Flats, it's for you, someone called

Rose,' announced a constable.'

'Hello Rose ….. Yes it's me ….. Really? ….. Okay, don't touch anything, leave everything as it is. I'll be with you within the hour ….. Thank you.' He put the phone down; 'We may have just gotten a breakthrough,' he announced as he left the room.

'Chief, I need a squad car and a couple of men; can I borrow Nick?' He then explained his reasons.

'We can do better than that, I'll come with you and yes, the Inspector can come too.'

'Give me a minute to have a word with Hoskins; I promised to take Willie back personally but I'm sure he'll understand if the Sergeant goes in my place.'

After a quick word with Hoskins, he informed Isla where he was going and told Andrea to grab her coat.

Chapter Sixteen

The Chief instructed Nick to get the keys for the Range Rover and bring it to the front of the building. As soon as they were all in the vehicle, Nick sped off.

'Would one of you mind telling me where we are going?' begged Nick.

'Kemble Farm, and don't hang about; use the lights and siren if necessary,' ordered the Chief.

Nick didn't need telling twice as he raced out of the town. Several times they came up behind slower moving vehicles and used the sirens to enable them to overtake. As they sped along the A37 towards Wraxall, Nick could see a couple of Lorries ahead of him. There was no way of getting past and the steepness of the incline slowed them to a crawl. At the top of the hill, he was able to pass the slow vehicles and accelerated towards Shepton Mallet. Twenty minutes later, he turned onto the familiar track leading to Kemble Farm. Seeing the vehicle arrive, Rose came to meet them. 'I do hope that I haven't wasted your time.'

'Not at all,' Flats assured her, 'now where is it exactly?'

She led the way to an area close to the racing stables. There was a shovel and a pitchfork lying on the ground; 'It's just over here; someone could have been hurt, we've been lucky.'

An elderly gentleman was sitting on an upturned wheelbarrow. 'This is Bert; he noticed it while he was bagging up some manure for his allotment.'

'You can see it just on the edge of the pile,' he said pointing.

On the ground was a discarded and empty syringe with the needle still attached to it. Nick put on a glove and very carefully placed the syringe in an evidence bag. 'What do you make of it Flats?'

'My first thought is that no professional vet would be so careless, it could be our first significant clue. I'm grateful Rose that you called us and not Bath station,' said Flats.

'Do you think we should have a poke around in the heap of manure?' asked Nick.

'It wouldn't hurt but be extremely careful; whilst you do that I want to have a look in the bins.'

Bert offered to help and Rose, wanting to do her bit, fetched a large rake. The Chief went with Flats and

Andrea and the three of them began checking the waste bins. 'Surely the forensic team would have searched through all this,' suggested Nick.

'Why would they?' replied Flats, 'until the autopsy had been done, none of us would have been looking for a syringe because the poor lad was obviously hanged. They would concentrate on footprints, tyre marks and anything that may have fallen from a pocket.'

'I think I might have something here,' said Andrea, 'can I have an evidence bag please?'

'What have you found?' asked Flats.

'It looks like an empty vial of some sort.' She carefully picked up the small glass container and bagged it. They continued to search the bins but found nothing else that was deemed significant. Flats suddenly went quiet and looked deep in thought. 'Chief; we need to bring a forensics team back here and preferably our own.'

'What's your reasoning for that?'

'Think about it, the syringe was discarded carelessly, so why discard a vial in the bin. It's more likely that it was thrown somewhere, possibly in this heap of manure. I could be wrong and the vial Andrea found may have contained the drug, but my gut is telling me different.'

'That's logical, I'll ask Rose if I can use a telephone to request that a team is dispatched with haste and I'll brief them accordingly.'

Flats then instructed Rose and Bert to refrain from searching further. 'Leave it to the experts; let's get this syringe back to Yeovil for Dicky to examine.'

When they returned to the station; Isla informed them that they now had artist impressions of the two men seen at Kemble Farm. 'The description given to us by Willie Wynne appears remarkably like one of them, so we have added the mug shots to our board.'

'Have we heard anything from the Jockey Club or Cheltenham station?' asked Flats.

'No, we're still waiting but they did promise to call the Sergeant later today with an update,' replied Isla.

'Very good, now I must call Dicky, we need his expertise to check the syringe and vial we found.'

The commissioner came into the room wanting an update. 'How is the investigation coming along?'

'We are making some progress,' Flats informed him, 'there are four clear suspects; unfortunately, there is not enough hard evidence at the moment. Finnegan smokes a certain brand of cigar and we have retrieved several butts from Kemble Farm, the scene where the horse was transferred after being abducted, and at Kenny's stable. All of these bear the same marks which were made by the tool used to clip the ends. Earlier we found a syringe at Kemble Farm which Dicky will be checking as soon as he gets here. If you look at our board, you will see artist drawings of two men, one of which claims to be a vet and the other a specialist horse breeder. One of these attempted to bribe Willie Wynne. I am hoping that we will identify both of them shortly.'

'Have you made any progress regarding the allegations of race fixing and betting irregularities?'

'Not yet but the team are trawling through all the financial information looking for clues. I will keep you informed of any developments as they happen.'

Sergeant Hoskins was in deep conversation on his telephone. When he put the receiver down he beckoned to Flats. 'We are in luck; the television crew has confirmed that they have a short clip of Sir Basil being led away from the stables. They are preparing some stills for us which should be ready in a couple of hours.'

'That is good news,' Flats paused for a moment, 'Sarge would you call them back and ask if they would confirm when they're ready. I think we should have them couriered to us or send someone to collect them. If they fax the pictures to us we may lose some of the clarity.'

'I'll phone them right away and then arrange for one of our motorcycle team to collect it.'

'It would seem that you're making good progress,' said the commissioner, 'keep it up.'

Dicky arrived, and after a brief chat with Flats said that he would get to work immediately. 'Can you spare my assistant to help me?'

'Oh I think the team can mange without her, she's all yours,' Flats replied.

Andrea was glad of the opportunity to help again and further her knowledge.

Flats handed Dicky the evidence bags containing the syringe and vial. He looked at them; 'Where, pray tell, did you find this?'

'In a large pile of horse poo,' replied Andrea, smiling.

'Charming, oh well let's get to it.'

As he stood back looking at the suspect board, Flats called to Isla. 'Have we no pictures of O'Donnell and Whelan?'

'Sorry but we've been concentrating on Finnegan, Nolan

and the two as yet unidentified men.'

'See if you can remedy this, and make sure we have several copies to show around. Hoskins, when is the next local race meeting? I'm thinking, Taunton, Wincanton, Salisbury or Bath ….. Or even Exeter.'

'Give me ten minutes and I'll get you a list.'

Flats went to the Chief Inspector's office; 'Is there any news from either of the other stations?'

'Not as yet, it seems that all the information we have is being passed to them, whereas nothing new is coming back to us.'

'Once we have the pictures from the TV Company, I want to visit a few stables to see if we can get a positive i.d. on any of our suspects. I want to try and track down the men who are offering the bribes.'

As they talked, Sergeant Hoskins entered; 'We're in luck Flats, Wincanton has a meeting in two days time.'

'Perfect; we need to be there and with a bit of luck, we may find some answers.'

Chapter Seventeen

Later in the day, a police dispatch rider collected some pictures and a small reel of film from the TV Company. On entering the station, he handed them over to Sergeant Hoskins. Dicky came into the incident room and triumphantly declared that they had managed to obtain several finger prints from the syringe and vial. 'That's the good news; the disappointing news is that they don't match. The vial contained an anti-biotic medicine.'

'That would suggest my hunch was right, let's hope the forensic team have better luck,' uttered Flats.

'I have a reel of film from the TV Company Flats,' announced Hoskins, 'give me ten minutes and I'll set it up for us to view. Here are the pictures they sent with it.'

Flats opened the envelope and laid the few pictures out on a table. 'Well, well, well, look at that; Mr. Nolan was present when Sir Basil was led away.' He selected one picture and held it up in front of his face. 'This is one of our mysterious men from Kemble Farm, but which one? Vet or Breeder?'

'I've got the projector set up Flats,' announced Hoskins.

'Very good Sergeant, let's have a look.'

The lights were dimmed and the projector whirred into life. They all watched the short clip of film which clearly showed the horse being led away. 'Can you run that again?' asked Flats. The film was re-started and he moved closer to the screen. 'There! Can you freeze it? Go back just a little; that's it. We need to get this frame converted to a picture and Lynne, check who was issued with pass number 437. My guess would be either Finnegan or Dolan.'

WPC Knott flicked through some papers; 'You're right as usual, that pass was issued to Mr. Finnegan care of the Shamrock Group.'

'How do you propose to find him?' asked Isla.

'Once we have a suitable photograph of him, I will first ask Aidan Lynch if he knows who it is. Chances are he can identify the individual and as you will all observe, he is also one of the two men from Kemble Farm. Hoskins, what happened to the sketch of the man based on Willie's description?'

'Sorry Flats, in all the excitement I forgot about that, it's there on my desk.'

'Andi, would you start a separate suspect board for our

race fixers? Include both Finnegan and Dolan; I am confident that we will find that they are involved.'

The Chief Inspector came to find Flats; 'I've been chatting with the commissioner and we think that we can actually charge someone for kidnapping their own property with the intention to deceive. Their actions affected the outcome of a race and it's possible they may have laid bets against their own horse. Either way, if you decide to make any arrests, you have our complete backing and support.'

'Thanks Chief, let me identify the man who led Sir Basil away first and then I might pursue that avenue. Would you arrange for the necessary warrants; just in case?'

Flats returned to the incident room where WPC Knott was eager to speak to him. 'We think that we've found something, look at these statements. They're Whelan and O'Donnell's personal bank accounts. I've highlighted certain cash transactions; there are quite a few of them.'

'I think that I should take a look at one of their dealerships because some of these could be for car purchases. Lynne, could you give me the addresses of the sites they own?'

Whilst she was jotting them down, a young constable approached with an envelope;

'Here you are sir; we've developed the film and got some clear pictures for you.'

'Thank you, that's good work. Andi, would you call Aidan Lynch and ask if he and Sean Kelly would meet us tomorrow at Kenny's stable? If they can, let Kenny know that we will be dropping by.'

Dicky said that as he was no longer required he would leave. 'I'll see you later Lynne; call me if you need me Flats, bye for now.'

Isla was curious; 'And what are you two doing later?' she probed.

'If you must know, Dicky is taking me and my daughter Megan, ten pin bowling.'

'Lucky you, I've never had a go at that.'

After making the calls, Andrea confirmed that everything was arranged for them to meet at Kenny's.

'Well there's nothing more to be done today we will re-convene in the morning.'

'Flats, just before you go; should I fax these photos to the other two stations?' asked Isla.

'Yes ….. But not until tomorrow afternoon,' he replied.

Later that evening; Isla came home looking really excited; 'The Chief informed me that I'm getting a new panda car next week, one of the Austin 1100's.'

Flats congratulated her; 'I should have mentioned earlier that Andi and I will be going to the stables first thing, and you'll be pleased to know that we have three eggs.'

~~~~

Armed with the photographs, Flats and Andrea drove to Kenny's stable. 'Good morning to you both; it's amazing that I don't see you for months and now you're a regular visitor to my stables. Come in to my office, we can sit and talk there. Willie has just given Honeycomb her morning ride and will join us shortly.'

When they were sat down, Flats opened an envelope and showed Kenny the pictures. He studied them carefully; 'Sorry my friend, I can't help you, I have seen the chap that offered a bribe to Willie, and the man leading Sir Basil away looks familiar; as for the third one, I've never seen him before.'

Willie joined them and was shown the pictures' he shook his head; 'Apart from the one I described I can't help you, I've never seen the other two.'

Flats looked frustrated; 'We have to hope that Aidan or

Sean can shed some light on these men. Do you have any horses running tomorrow at Wincanton Kenny?'

'Actually I have two, Honeycomb and Trapezium; both are showing well on the gallops.'

'I'm hoping to ride a double,' said Willie, 'so if you don't need me anymore then I need to exercise a couple more horses.'

Flats thanked him and said that they would be in touch if they needed further assistance.

'What did he mean by 'ride a double'?' Andrea asked.

'It means he's hoping to win both races, hence the double,' replied Kenny.

'We're going to be at Wincanton so maybe I'll have a flutter on them,' said Andrea.

A car drove into the yard and two familiar gentlemen got out and came to the office. They all exchanged pleasantries before Flats showed them the pictures. Both men looked concerned as they checked them.

'The guy leading Sir Basil away is Finnegan's son Niall, nasty piece of work,' informed Sean.

Aidan held up one picture; 'Niall is nothing compared to

138

this guy,' he offered, 'that's Frank Brennan; better known as Frank the Fly. He owns a couple of betting shops which are really a front for dubious activities. The other person is one of his boys ….. What's his name?'

'I believe that's Bill McCann, or Billy the 'Bung' as he's known,' answered Sean.

'Why is he known as Frank the Fly?' enquired Andrea.

'Young lady, have you heard of the saying that I'd like to be a fly on the wall? Well this man has a way of finding information that suggests he's just that when a discussion is taking place. He has ears and eyes in so many places,' explained Aidan.

'If you're going after this guy Flats, tread very carefully, you could end up supporting a motorway bridge somewhere,' warned Sean.

'Thanks for the warning but someone murdered a young jockey and one or more of these men could well be involved. At least two of your former syndicate has something to do with it too. I will bring whoever is responsible to justice, mark my words.'

'I expected you would say that,' said Aidan as he reached inside his jacket. 'Here are our personal numbers for you and you only, if you need some ….. Shall we say unofficial assistance, if you get my drift; give us a call. Now, as our business here is concluded, we will be on our way.'

'We'd better get going too, thank you all for your help,' said Flats.

As they headed to the station, Andrea was feeling uneasy; 'Aren't you scared?'

'My dear girl, we all get a little frightened at times but the warnings serve as a reminder to be extra vigilant. I'll understand if you would prefer to stay at home during this investigation.'

'I admit that I feel a little worried but there's no way you're doing this alone. Someone has to watch your back, and that 'someone' is me.'

Chapter Eighteen

As they arrived at the station, Flats noticed Dicky's car parked at the front. 'I didn't expect to see him this morning.'

'Perhaps he's come to see Lynne,' teased Andrea.

When they entered the incident room, Flats looked for his friend; 'Does anyone know where Dicky is?'

'He's in the evidence room,' answered Isla, 'believe it or not, the forensics team found a vial near the heap of manure and he's busy looking for prints. How did your trip go?'

'We have names for all three men,' said Andrea, 'I'm just going to put them on the board.'

'I will need background checks on them as soon as possible. Andi, can you keep Jeeves with you while I have a word with the Chief.'

'Good morning Larry; we have names for the three suspects. The man who led the horse away from the stables at Cheltenham was Niall Finnegan, son of Seamus. He is also one of the two seen at Kemble Farm so I want to bring him in for questioning. As he isn't an owner of Sir Basil, I believe we can arrest him for kidnapping or abduction. Do you think that we can stretch a point and arrest his father and Dara Nolan?'

'Let me check with the commissioner. You realise that Bath will be responsible for making the actual arrests. We can of course assist them if requested, and I'm sure the commissioner will persuade them to do so.'

'I was warned that this Niall is a nasty piece of work and the man seen with him at Kemble Farm is Frank Brennan. Apparently he's even worse; my hunch is that he was involved with the killing of Ben Collis.'

'I've heard Brennan's name mentioned before but we can't arrest him unless we have some kind of evidence. He will no doubt have a top lawyer so please proceed with caution,' warned the Chief.

'I will; we're going to Wincanton tomorrow to speak to the jockeys, I want to know how many have been offered bribes by Billy McCann. Our sources suggest that he's one of the main culprits in offering incentives for them to throw races.'

'Okay Flats, take whoever you need, including Nick if you want and I'll talk to the commissioner.'

Dicky had completed his checks on the vial and informed Flats that he was able to extract several prints. 'One of them is a perfect match to one found on the syringe.'

'How are we going to find out whose prints they are?' queried Andrea.

'Dicky, what do you reckon to the old 'going to search for it' ruse?'

'That might work Flats; in any case it's certainly worth trying.

The others in the room look puzzled; 'It will all become clear very soon,' offered Dicky.

Flats turned to Nick; 'I would like you to accompany us tomorrow when we go to Wincanton. In the meantime, can you make sure that Bath receives copies of the pictures we have. Then speak to the D.I. and request they conduct discreet surveillance on the abattoir to see if any of the suspects go there.'

'How long shall I tell them to watch the place?'

'Just for a couple of days; we will be paying a visit to the abattoir in a day or two, but you don't need to tell him that. Sarge, fancy a trip to the races?'

'I would love one, what time are we leaving?'

'Probably around nine, the first race isn't until the afternoon which will give us plenty of time to speak to the jockeys.'

'Would you like me to come along too?' asked Dicky.

Flats thought for a moment; 'Yes, that would be helpful, you can team up with Sergeant Hoskins. It would be ideal if you take your car, if that's okay with you.'

'Of course, we don't want us all to arrive at the same time in a group.'

'Exactly my thoughts; Nick, you and Isla will go together and that just leaves Andrea and me. That should be enough of us as we don't want to arouse suspicions. We'll meet here around eight thirty.'

As Flats was preparing to leave, the Chief caught up with him. 'I thought you should know that the arrest warrants have been issued for all the suspects.'

'Thanks Chief; tomorrow we'll go to Wincanton and then, probably the day after, we'll be making some arrests. To that end I have a plan which I will inform you about in due course. We'll discuss it when we return from the trip to the racecourse.'

The following morning, everyone met up at the station in preparation for the day ahead. Flats suggested that Nick and Isla should leave first followed by Dicky and Hoskins about ten minutes later. 'We, Andi, will leave a further ten minutes after that.'

When Nick and Isla arrived they mingled with the crowds as they tried to blend in. Some of the tic-tac men were setting up their posts and writing the horses and their odds on chalk boards. 'We should get a couple of programs, so that we blend in,' suggested Nick.

After parking up, Dicky and Hoskins went straight for the parade ring. There were a couple of stable lads walking horses around for gentle exercise but it was still relatively quiet. 'Perhaps we should check out the hospitality tents,' said Dicky.

Flats and Andrea made their way directly to the stables to find Kenny. Willie spotted them and came to say hello. 'Would you like to see my two mounts for today?'

'Yes please,' replied Andrea excitedly.

'Where's Kenny?' asked Flats.

'He went to get a couple of teas, he'll be back shortly.'

They followed Willie to the stables; 'This is Honeycomb and the grey over there is Trapezium.'

'You told us the other day that you fancy your chances with both of them, is that still the case?'

Willie nodded; 'Definitely, they both went well on the gallops earlier.'

'We've got to have a flutter,' said Andrea.

'Just remember young lady that we are here on business. Tell me Willie, have you seen either of these men around this morning?' questioned Flats and showing the pictures he had with him.

'No I haven't, but it's still early.'

'Are there any jockeys around here that you know personally?' asked Flats.

'There are a couple; one moment, HEY CHAS! Have you got a minute?' He called out.

A jockey strode across the yard to them; 'These are a couple of friends of mine, Flats and Andrea; they would like to ask you a couple of questions.'

'Sure, what would you like to know?'

'Have you seen either of these men today? Especially this one.' Flats asked, pointing to a picture of Billy McCann.

'I haven't seen them today but that one offered me some money a while back to throw a race. He made it quite clear that if I didn't, my family would suffer. I got lucky that day; three fences from home a loose horse cut across us forcing me to pull up. By the time we got going again the others were too far ahead. Please don't inform the authorities, I could lose my licence.'

'Thank you for the information, and don't worry, your secret is safe with us.' Flats assured him.

As Chas walked away, something caught Andrea's eye. She gave a gentle tug on Flats' arm and rolled her eyes in the direction of the stables further up the yard. There was a man dressed in a long brown coat and following at a reasonable distance was Dicky and Hoskins. The man entered one of the stables causing both Dicky and Hoskins to quicken their pace. Flats, realising that something wasn't right, moved swiftly to join them. Suddenly a voice called out; 'OY YOU, WHAT DO YOU THINK YOU'RE DOING?'

The man in the brown coat came running out of the stable followed by a young girl; he brushed past Dicky sending him sprawling. As he ran towards Flats, he attempted to slow him down. Hoskins was now in full flight and gaining fast as the man raced past Andrea. A few more yards and the Sergeant hurled himself full stretch like a rugby player and brought the fleeing man crashing to the ground. There was a painful grunt as Hoskins landed on the man which was followed by a high pitch scream, and the two men lay motionless. Flats aided by both Andrea and Dicky, rolled Hoskins off the man who had been knocked unconscious by the tackle. They could then see what had caused the loud scream. Sticking out of the side of Hoskins was a syringe and the fall had caused the needle to bend. For a brief moment there was a smile on his face before his body went totally limp and his eyes closed. Dicky reached for his handkerchief and removed the syringe.

'Someone is going to have a headache in the morning. He's lucky that he only got part of the dose because I suspect that this contains some type of sedating drug.'

Flats told Andrea to find Nick and Isla or a policeman. 'We need some handcuffs and we'd better get an ambulance for poor Hoskins.'

It wasn't long before the emergency vehicle arrived and Hoskins was loaded onto a stretcher and taken away for treatment. Andrea had come back with Nick and Isla and the unconscious man was handcuffed.

'Do either of you have any gloves?' asked Flats.

Isla opened her bag and gave him a pair. Flats put them

on and then rifled through the man's pockets where he found a small bottle. Isla had also produced an evidence bag in readiness for any suspicious items. With the bottle safely in the bag, Dicky asked to have a look at it. Andrea sidled up to him to see what it was.

'Diazepam,' she said out loud, 'that's one of the Benzodiazepine drugs. No wonder the Sergeant is out cold, they are sedatives. You're right Dicky, he's very lucky he didn't get the full dose.'

'Hang on a minute Andi; this bottle is full, so where did the contents of the syringe come from?'

By now the man was beginning to stir. A police car pulled up and Flats ordered the officers to escort the suspect to the station and hold him for questioning. As soon as he was bundled into the car and taken away, Flats went to the stable where the man had been accosted. There was a young girl inside tending to a horse.

'Excuse me miss, are you okay?'

'Yes thank you, that man dropped this,' she said handing over a small empty bottle.

Flats took out his handkerchief and took it from her. 'Can you tell me whose horse this is and its name?'

'His name is Bramble and he's owned by the haulage company of Brown and Sons. He's the overwhelming favourite for the third race today,' she replied.

'Thank you,' said Flats, he went outside, 'Okay; now that we're all here we may as well work through the jockeys and trainers as our cover is blown. Dicky, I have an empty bottle which the man dropped in the stable. That should solve your conundrum as to where the liquid in the syringe came from.'

Chapter Nineteen

Kenny came back to his stable carrying a couple of cups and Willie informed him of the excitement whilst he was gone. The two of them watched as Flats and his team spoke to everyone else in the stabling area.

Nick summoned Flats to come and speak to another jockey. 'This gentleman has also been offered money to throw a race by Billy McCann.'

'Good work Nick; take his details and get a statement; and would you find Willie's friend Chas and make a note of his details too. Andi, can you find some water to give

Jeeves a drink, me and Dicky are going for a wander.'

'Okay pops, where will I find you?'

Flats shook his head and held out his hand in the dog's direction. 'Jeeves will lead you to me.'

'Silly me, I wasn't thinking,' said Andrea.

'Who or what are we looking for,' queried Dicky.

'I don't believe that the man we've arrested is here on his own. My guess is that at least one of our three suspects is somewhere on the course.'

'The place is beginning to fill up; they won't be easy to spot.'

'I agree that it's a long shot with just the two of us but you never know.'

As they strolled through the crowds, Andrea caught up with them. 'Any luck?'

'Unfortunately no; I think it's time to leave and go back to the station via a brief stop at the hospital. Hopefully Hoskins will have woken from his induced slumber. After we've finished there, I would like to check on Stirling's warehouse to see what progress has been made.'

When they found Hoskins, he was sitting up in bed but looking a little sleepy. Andrea sat on the edge of the bed; 'Haven't you got anything better to do than lie around Sarge?' she teased.

'That's terrible Andi, he's had enough needle for one day,' joked Flats.

'Leave her alone, she's only trying to inject a little humour into the situation,' tormented Dicky.

Hoskins managed a forced smile before he nodded off. 'We'd better go and let him sleep,' suggested Flats.

After checking with the doctor's to ascertain that the Sergeant would be fine, they drove to the station. 'Nick; can you have our suspect taken to an interview room? Isla I want you there too, taking notes.'

The Chief wanted an account of the day.

'Let me question this man in custody and then I'll give you a full report.' promised Flats, 'by the way, do we have a name for our suspect?'

'According to him, his name is Jack Dawe; WPC Knott is running background checks to see if he is known to us or has a criminal record.'

'We're ready when you are Flats; the suspect is in

interview room one,' said Nick.

Flats and Nick sat together on one side of the table with Jack Dawe opposite. Isla sat separately with pen poised to take notes. After the formal introductions Nick began the questioning.

'Who are you working for and where did you get the drugs?'

'No comment,' came the reply.

'How did you get to the racecourse?'

'No comment.'

'We're wasting our time Nick,' said Flats angrily, 'have him taken back to the cells and ask Dicky to take his finger prints, we'll charge him later. I'm going to check with Lynne to see if she's found anything.'

'This was one of the easiest suspects to trace. Jack Dawe has previous convictions, mainly for burglary and petty theft. There's no way that he's acting alone because this is way above his normal M.O.' Lynne reported.

'Keep digging to see if you can connect him to any one of the other suspects. I'll be with the Chief if you find something.'

'Ah Flats, I had Bath on the phone earlier, they've been holding Deidre Finnegan and wanted to know if they can release her as she's not been charged. I instructed them to keep her in custody and charge her for receiving stolen goods. That should buy us some time.'

'I've just had a thought chief; she's related to Seamus and she owns Kemble Farm. They would possibly have certain drugs on site, it's a long shot but worth checking. I wanted to make some arrests tomorrow but we'll hold off for the time being. This is what I propose we do.' Flats went on to explain his plan.

'Very clever, that might just work. Oh, I've spoken to the hospital; Hoskins will be released in the morning. The effects of the drug should have completely worn off by then. I told him to take a couple days off to fully recover but knowing him, I bet he'll be at his desk before you know it.'

'Can you spare Nick tomorrow? I think it best if just the two of us go. I'll leave you to take care of the other side of things; I'm calling it a day here soon as I have a planned visit elsewhere.' He quickly returned to the incident room where Dicky approached him.

'We have lifted several prints from the syringe and the two bottles. Andi suggested that we check against those found at Kemble Farm, and you'll never believe it, we found a match. Before you ask, no, it's not Mr. Dawe's on both, we still have to determine who the other's belong to.'

'Jack Dawe is not answering our questions at the moment but he will be charged in due course. I thank you all for your good work and will see you sometime tomorrow. Nick, if it's okay with you, I would like to leave here around nine.'

'I'll be ready and waiting,' he replied.

Flats and Andrea drove to Stirling's warehouse. The old fence had been removed and the new higher one was being erected. Work had begun on the new security office and the footings were complete. As he entered the compound, a car drove past them. A shudder ran down Flats' spine; 'Did you see who that was?'

'Sorry pops, I wasn't really paying attention. I was too busy looking at the work. Who was it?'

'Unless I'm mistaken, that was Frank Brennan.' He spun around in his seat and looked back as the car turned out of the site. He reached into his pocket and took out a pen. As he didn't have a piece of paper he wrote the car's registration on his hand. 'We need to tread very carefully and watch what we say while we're here,' warned Flats.

'Knowing what we do about Brennan, could he be involved in some sort of smuggling as well?' implied Andrea.

'That's a distinct possibility; the big question is whether Stirling is involved with him or is he ignorant of exactly who Frank Brennan is.'

'There's only one way to find out, let's go and talk to the man himself.'

They found Stirling in his office; 'Good afternoon Flats, Andrea, this is a pleasant surprise. Have you come to check on the progress?'

'Yes we have, and I must admit that I didn't expect to see so much improvement. Tell me, was that Frank Brennan I saw leaving?'

'It was; do you know him? He's going to be one of my first customers. The builders are sending a full team to work on the security building and the CCTV Company has already begun to lay the necessary cables. Hopefully, we might just be ready within our original time scale.'

'That's good news; we won't take up any more of your time but before we go, do you mind if we take a look around the site?'

'Be my guests, you don't need to ask and I'll hope to see

you again soon.'

Once they were outside, Andrea wanted Flats' opinion on whether Stirling knew who Frank really was.

'To be honest, I'm not sure but it begs the question; why does he want to do business so far from his home? Your original assessment may be correct, either way; he's up to no good, that's for sure.'

After a thorough check of the whole site, and being satisfied with the progress, they left and headed home.

Chapter Twenty

The following morning when Flats entered the police station, he was surprised to see Hoskins back at work. 'Good morning Sarge, I guess you can't keep a good man down. Nice to see you, are you sure your okay?'

'I just needed to sleep it off; where's miss cheeky chops?'

'She'll be along shortly with Isla; I need to make some arrangements. Do you feel up to a field trip later?'

'Oh yes; if the Chief says it's okay then count me in.'

Flats went to the incident room where he found Nick checking over the case files with WPC Knott. 'Good morning you two; have we got all the arrest warrants here that I requested?'

Nick handed him a file; 'All in here, so who are we bringing in today?'

'I want to bring in Finnegan's son Niall; would you mind checking in with Bath to see if he's at the abattoir? And if that's the case, inform them that I want D.I. Phelps present for any arrests. Ask them where we can meet discreetly; I don't want to spook anyone.'

Dicky arrived; 'Is everything in place for today?'

'I believe so but I've not briefed the others of our plan just yet. There will only be four of us going to the abattoir. We will be leaving shortly, after I've spoken to the Chief.'

'What's all the cloak and dagger stuff Flats? I would like to know your plan.'

'Of course Larry, you ought to let the commissioner know; I'm sure he will want to be informed.' He then explained his idea and asked if he could enlist the help of Nick.

'Of course you can; how many others will you require?'

'Just two, to accompany Isla and Andrea.'

When the two girls came into the incident room, Flats gave Isla instructions to call Bath and have Sergeant Williams, and a team of his officers, to meet her at Kemble Farm. He then handed her a couple of items in evidence bags; 'You know what to do with these.'

After receiving confirmation that Niall Finnegan was indeed at the abattoir, Flats addressed the team.

'If everyone is ready, we should go. Andi, keep Jeeves with you, I'll see you later.'

She came over to him and kissed him on the cheek; 'Please be careful.'

On the way to the abattoir, Nick questioned Flats about his plan but he was told to be patient and all would become apparent in due course. As they neared their destination, they met with D.I. Phelps and his officers at the pre-arranged rendezvous point.

'What do you want us to do?' he asked.

'I want you and your team to seal off the entrances in case Niall Finnegan tries to make a run for it. My gut feeling is that he won't come without some resistance.

Okay Nick, let's go.'

They drove up the lane to the main building of the abattoir. A security guard stopped them and asked what they wanted. Nick flashed his badge; 'Police business, we're here to see Mr. Finnegan.'

'I'll let him know you're here, you can park near the main entrance,' said the guard as he allowed them in.

Dara Nolan met them in the reception area; 'Hello gents, I understand that you would like to see my partner; follow me please.'

He led them to an office where Seamus Finnegan was sat behind a large antique desk. He rose to his feet and looked at Flats; 'We've met before, you're the private investigator chap, Magull something.'

'It's Flats Magull; this is D.I. Nick Crookes and we're here to speak to your son Niall.'

'Would you mind telling me what this is all about?'

'Certainly; on the day that your horse was removed from Cheltenham racecourse, we have film evidence showing your son leading him away. As the horse did not belong to him, that's kidnapping. He has also been seen at Kemble Farm, which as you know was where the jockey known as Ben Collis was found hanging from a beam.'

'So he's been to Kemble Farm, that's no crime. The jockey committed suicide,' snapped Finnegan.

'Ben Collis was murdered; Dicky Martin here is a pathologist, and he found a needle mark on the neck under the noose. The poor jockey was heavily sedated before he was strung up. It's our assumption that the syringe used was likely discarded at the farm. We have a team of forensics going there in the morning to conduct a thorough search, now where is your son?'

Out the corner of his eye, Flats noticed someone in the corridor. There was the sound of running footsteps followed by a door slamming. 'Come on Nick, he's making a run for it.'

When they got outside, Hoskins had spotted Niall running away and gave chase. Before he could get anywhere near him, the fleeing suspect got into his car and sped up the track used by the Lorries. As he neared the exit, he saw a police car blocking his way out. Making a sharp turn he realised that Nick, in his car, was cutting off his way back. For a moment it looked as though he was trapped. Niall accelerated hard and crashed through the fencing and headed across the grass towards the second entrance. A second police car was now parked blocking his escape route there. He then ploughed through a hedge and drove across the field beyond. By now the first police car, followed by Nick, was driving along the road adjacent to the field. The second police car was now giving pursuit over the bumpy terrain. In his effort to shake off the pursuing police car, Niall was pushing his car to its limits. The uneven ground was shaking his vehicle but he was unperturbed. Realising that his escape route via the main road was blocked, he turned sharply away from it. As he did so, his rear wheels dug into the ground and for a moment he was stuck. Niall pressed the accelerator right to the floor and suddenly the tyres gripped the ground causing his car to shoot forward. There was a slight mound and as he drove over it, the front of the car dipped forcefully down crashing into the earth. The sudden jolt meant that the engine had stalled and the car was stuck. Niall climbed out of the car and made a dash for it. Two officers from the pursuing car were swiftly out and giving chase. Flats and the others had stopped and were watching from the road. Although Niall had a good head start, one of the officers was gaining fast. D.I. Phelps informed Flats and the others that constable Bates was a cross country running enthusiast. 'He'll catch him easily,' he boasted.

It wasn't long before Bates caught up with Niall and tackled him. There was a brief scuffle before the second officer arrived and the two of them pinned him to the ground. They then handcuffed him, dragged him to his feet, and marched him to the waiting officers.

'Have you read him his rights?' asked D.I. Phelps.

'No sir, I wasn't sure what the charges are,' replied Bates.

'Niall Finnegan, I am arresting you for the offence of kidnapping a horse and resisting arrest,' announced the D.I. before reading him his rights. 'I want him taken to Yeovil for questioning,' demanded Flats. 'If you can arrange that please, we need to go to Kemble Farm.'

Isla and Andrea had arrived at the farm and met up with Sergeant Williams and his team. 'The first thing that we have to do is to conceal these vehicles and then find places for us to hide,' instructed Isla.

She then spoke to the two policemen who were guarding the farm. 'Has anyone tried to gain access?' she asked.

'No ma'am, the only people who have been here was the lady who runs the riding school and one lorry to take away the last two horses. They were here at the same time.'

She then informed them that they may receive a couple of visitors and to refuse them entry. 'Should they turn up and get nasty, don't endanger yourselves.

Chapter Twenty One

Flats arrived at Kemble Farm to be met by Andrea and Isla. 'We've made a place for you to hide your car around the far side of the stables,' said Isla.

'Have you been able to check the drugs cabinet?'

'Not yet; it's locked and Rose says that she doesn't have access to it so we can't check its contents.'

Dicky looked at Flats; 'I bet it hasn't been properly secured,' he said with a wry smile.

'That was my thought too; we should take a look for ourselves,' replied Flats.

He gave instructions to Nick to hide the car and then find a suitable surveillance spot. 'Do you believe that someone will turn up?' asked Nick.

'If either Finnegan or Dolan had any involvement, then yes, I think they will. Now, what say we take a look at this drugs cabinet?'

As Nick drove the car to its hiding place, Flats, Dicky and Hoskins walked over to the office.

'That's not a very secure looking padlock,' said Flats, reaching inside his jacket pocket. 'I think you should look away Hoskins.'

'Oh I shouldn't worry Flats, my eyesight is not that good and the memory can be fuzzy at times.'

'Well would you look at that; someone didn't close the padlock properly. Do you have any gloves Dicky?'

'Yes of course; one moment.' He handed over a pair and took out an evidence bag.

Flats looked at the drugs and medicines in the cupboard before taking out a couple of small bottles. 'I'm sure this is the same batch number as the one we found, and the syringes are definitely the same type.' He carefully removed a few bottles and syringes; 'You'll need to dust these for prints, we need to see if anyone other than Deidre Finnegan has handled these.'

Nick joined them in the office; 'Is there anything specific that you want me to do?'

'Just check on the placement of all the officers on site and make sure they are aware of what's expected. No one makes a move until I give the word. We ought to take our places too, if my hunch is right, we can expect company fairly soon.'

As the time ticked by, the tension at the farm mounted. They had been waiting for over an hour when a Brown Ford Zodiac car approached the farm. It stopped at the entrance where the duty policemen informed them that the farm was off limits to the public. The man in the passenger seat got out and produced a gun. Flats immediately recognised that it was Dara Nolan.

'I don't think you understand; we wish to enter.'

Both policemen backed off to allow the car access. A second vehicle had pulled up behind the Zodiac and four men got out. Under Nolan's instruction, they grabbed the frightened officers and bound their hands together.

'Put them in one of the stables,' he ordered, and then join us.'

Flats looked at the team around him and shook his head; 'Don't any of you try to be a hero, they are armed and dangerous,' he whispered.

They watched as Nolan and Finnegan instructed the other men where to look. For almost an hour they diligently sifted through the pile of manure and combed the surrounding area. Eventually, one of the men shouted out and held up a small bottle; 'Is this what we're looking for?'

Finnegan took the object and looked at it; 'That's one of the items but there should be a syringe somewhere.' He then dropped the bottle on to the ground and raised his foot; in one swift movement he stamped heavily on it, causing it to smash into numerous pieces. Again and again he stomped on the bits of glass until all that remained were shattered remnants. When he was satisfied, he scattered the tiny remains using his foot. Shortly afterwards; the syringe was found and put in a bag. Nolan then ordered the men to leave.

'What do you want us to do about the cops in the stable?' asked one of the men.

'Go and get their number badges and warn them that we can find out where they live,' replied Nolan, 'tell them if they keep quiet their families won't get hurt, then get out of here.'

With Nolan back in the passenger seat, Finnegan drove off at speed. A few minutes later the second car also sped off.

Flats emerged from his hiding place and the team gathered around him. 'I commend you all for remaining concealed and not trying any heroics; I was not expecting them to be armed. Can someone go and untie the poor policemen in the stable?'

Sergeant Williams and one of his constables walked over to the stable. Moments later he came out and shouted for someone to call an ambulance. Everyone rushed to the stable and were shocked to discover that both policemen had been shot. 'We never heard any shots,' said Nick.

'They probably used silencers to mask the sound,' replied Flats. 'D.I. Phelps, get the rest of your men back to your station and have them give descriptions to a sketch artist. Isla, you do the same with your colleagues at Yeovil, we need to identify these killers. Nick, D.I. Phelps, Dicky and I will wait for the ambulance and additional officers. Has anyone got a couple of evidence bags and some gloves?'

'I have Flats, you know I carry a supply,' answered Dicky, 'now let's see if we can find any clues.'

A young policeman came into the stable, 'I've radioed for an ambulance and extra officers; they'll be here soon.'

After everyone had left, Dicky took a look at the dead bodies. 'At least this is straightforward, single bullet to the head in both cases. We need to see if we can find the bullets and any spent casings.'

Using all his knowledge and expertise, Dicky tried to calculate the position of the men when they were shot.

After much deliberation, he pointed to an area;

'Somewhere around here is where the projectiles would have landed,' he intimated, drawing a circle in the air with his hand.

They all scrutinized the area with great care; 'I think I've found a bullet embedded here,' cried Nick.

As the others continued searching, Dicky inspected the spot and nodded; 'That looks like one of them; I need to get a knife to dig it out of the wood.'

'It doesn't look as though there are any bullet shells,' announced D.I. Phelps.

'That narrows down the choice of gun used,' said Dicky.

'I believe I have found the second bullet,' said Hoskins.

As they retrieved the object; the ambulance arrived followed by two police cars. Flats informed the medics about the two bodies whilst D.I. Phelps spoke to the attending officers. After taking many pictures of the scene, Dicky gave permission for the bodies to be taken away. 'My work is finished here,' he declared.

Flats beckoned to Nick and the two of them went to the office. Picking up the receiver of the phone, Flats dialled ….. Hello, can you put me through to the Chief Inspector

….. Yes, tell him it's Flats and it's urgent ….. Ah, Isla's told you ….. Okay Larry, we'll be with you shortly.'

Dicky and Hoskins joined them in the office. 'The Chief has already spoken to the commissioner and arrest warrants will be issued for both Nolan and Finnegan forthwith. Armed units have been put on high alert to bring them in. As soon as we can identify the other men, they will be arrested too. Now let me have a word with D.I. Phelps and then we can go.'

Chapter Twenty Two

They arrived back at Yeovil police station where the commissioner was waiting with the Chief Inspector. 'Ah Flats, DS White has given us an account of the events at Kemble Farm. The loss of two promising young officers is tragic and very disconcerting; I will need a report from you. Do you have any idea why they were shot?'

'No commissioner, it doesn't make sense; We heard that the criminals were ordered to collect their badges and threaten them, but there was no command to shoot them.'

'Well, because of what has transpired, I have commissioned a specialist armed unit, led by Chief Superintendent Yeates, who is ready to go on my command. We have surveillance teams at the houses of both Finnegan and Nolan. As soon as they confirm that the thugs are in their relevant homes, we'll send in the armed unit to make the arrest.'

'Thank you commissioner; do we know how the artist impressions are coming along?' asked Flats.

'Ask DS White, she's handling that,' said the Chief.

Flats went to the incident room where Isla was coordinating the sketches. 'What do you think of these?'

'Very accurate, this one is a very good likeness of one of the killers. Trying to put names to them is the next step, and will prove difficult.'

'Why not ask Aidan Lynch or Sean Kelly if they can identify them?' asked Andrea.

'That's not a bad idea, replied Flats, 'Nick, would you liaise with your oppo at Bath and ask him to fax through their photo fits as soon as possible. Make sure we return the compliment, who knows; maybe they will identify these low lifes before we do.'

The Chief Inspector rushed into the room; 'We've got

word that Finnegan is at his home; the command has been given to the armed unit who will be there shortly. Bath has informed me that Deidre Finnegan's lawyer turned up at the station demanding her release. Although Dicky only found a couple of partial prints on the bottle, which he has attributed to her, she has now been charged as an accessory-after-the-fact along with receiving stolen goods. It's enough to hold her for now.'

'I think it's time to have a word with Niall Finnegan. Isla, would you and Sergeant Hoskins have him taken to an interview room, let's see what he has to say.'

Flats asked Nick if he had spoken to Bath station. 'Yes and they will fax their results shortly.'

'Good, if you are free, I would like you to accompany me and instigate the interrogation of Finnegan junior.'

Flats briefed Nick as to what he should ask before they entered the room. 'I'll step in when I think it's appropriate.'

After the necessary introductions, Nick began the interrogation; 'Can you tell me why you took Sir Basil away from its stable?'

'I don't know what you're talking about.'

Isla produced a photograph; 'This was taken on the day

the horse disappeared, and that's you. We also have some film footage that corroborates this.'

'So you have pictures of me with my dad's horse, so what?'

'The horse was owned by a consortium of which your dad was a member,' said Flats, 'so where did you take the horse, because it wasn't returned to its stable?'

'I can't remember, I think I gave it to someone else.'

'Would that someone else have been either your dad or Mr. Nolan?' asked Nick.

There was no reply as Niall fell silent.

'Okay; let's move on, why were you seen at Kemble Farm in the vicinity of where Sir Basil was found?'

'My aunt owns the place and I was visiting.'

'Then tell me what Frank Brennan was doing there as he was with you on more than one occasion.'

Niall Finnegan's face changed to a worried frown.

'According to staff at the farm, you were both there several times after the horse was taken. What's your connection to Frank Brennan?'

Once again there was silence; Flats gave Nick a knowing glance and discreetly held up his thumb.

'It's our belief that both of you were involved in the abduction of the horse for financial gain; probably for laying bets on another horse in the race that he was supposed to run in ….. Perhaps we should let it be known that you told us of Brennan's involvement.'

'NO; he would kill me, you can't do that.'

Nick stood up; 'That's it, interview suspended, take him back to his cell.'

'I want my lawyer, you can't use such lies,' protested Finnegan as he was led away.

'I'm impressed,' congratulated Flats.

'It's a trick that I learnt from the master,' he replied with a grin, 'leave him to stew for a while, he's obviously scared of Brennan.'

~~~~

The armed unit cautiously approached the residence of Seamus Finnegan. C.S. Yeates surveyed the surrounding area; thankfully the house was a large detached building set in extensive grounds. A telecoms van drove into the road and stopped by a telegraph pole. Two men got out and erected a small barrier around the base. One of them put on his safety gear and began climbing the pole. Once he was near the top, he nodded to the Superintendent. After a final check; three armed officers were given the order to go to the rear of the property. When he was satisfied they were in place, he approached the front door with a couple of armed men and rang the door bell. It was Seamus Finnegan in person who answered the door. As soon as he saw the men, he slammed the door and raced to the back of the house. This was the cue for the man at the top of the telegraph pole to cut a wire. Finnegan called to his wife; 'Ring Nolan and warn him.' He grabbed his handgun and tore out of the back door. Before he'd got ten yards, he was confronted by the armed officers.

'Put down your weapon and kneel on the ground,' shouted one of the men.

For a brief moment, Finnegan considered his options before he sunk to his knees and dropped the handgun to the ground. One of the officers walked around Finnegan, kicking the gun away in the process, and ordered him to put his hands behind his back. He was very roughly man handled and handcuffed before being led away protesting his innocence. The handgun was retrieved and placed in an evidence bag.

~~~~

Back at Yeovil station, the Chief's phone rang; after a brief conversation, he went to the incident room.

'I have just spoken to Chief Superintendent Yeates; they have Finnegan in custody and he is being brought here as we speak. They are now heading to Nolan's home in anticipation; hopefully it won't be too long before we have him as well.'

Dicky entered the room with a frustrated frown; 'Finnegan junior is refusing to allow me to take his finger prints.'

'Oh is he? Hoskins; would you grab a couple of men to help 'persuade' Mr. Finnegan to co-operate.'

'I would be delighted to Chief,' replied Hoskins smiling.

Flats was looking at the photo fit sketches; 'I have spoken to Aidan Lynch and he's agreed to meet me later at one of his restaurants. I am hoping he may know one or two of these criminals.'

'Will you require an officer to accompany you?' offered the Chief.

'I don't think that will be necessary, but thanks for the offer, Andi and I can handle it; besides, you need all your staff here to help crack this case.'

WPC Knott called to Flats; 'I think we've identified one of the men as a Roger Locke. We're just trying to get some background information on him.'

'Well done, that's a good start. It's a shame he wasn't actually one of the killers,' said Flats.

'I will assign a couple more staff to assist the team; the commissioner has insisted that this case is our top priority. If you need me further, I will be in my office.'

Dicky returned with Andrea and a smirking Sergeant Hoskins. 'We now have Niall Finnegan's prints, thanks to the Sergeant.'

'Andi, you and I have a meeting with Aidan later, and I believe it includes a meal.'

'Ooh, sounds nice; do you think that I should change for the occasion?'

Before Flats could answer, the Chief rushed in smiling; 'The armed unit have arrested Dara Nolan. Apparently they arrived just as he returned to his house and nicked him as he got out of his car.'

'Hold them overnight and we'll question them in the morning. Let them get a feel of what incarceration feels like,' said Flats mischievously. Now if you'll excuse me, I have a dinner date to attend, see you all tomorrow.'

Chapter Twenty Three

Flats and Andrea journeyed to the designated restaurant; 'Do you think they'll allow Jeeves in?' asked Andrea.

'I'm sure Aidan won't mind, anyway, he's not being left in the car.'

When they arrived, Andrea was impressed by the imposing building; 'I wasn't expecting this.'

'The restaurant is inside the Hotel; you don't have to be a resident to dine here.' Picking up the file from the back seat of the car, Flats got out; 'Come on boy.' Jeeves didn't need telling twice and, following at his master's side, they all entered the building.

A suited gentleman greeted them; 'Good evening sir, you must be Mr. Magull, would you come with me please.'

They followed him into the restaurant and to a specific

table; 'Please make yourselves comfortable whilst I inform Mr. Lynch of your arrival.'

Several minutes later both Aidan Lynch and Sean Kelly came and sat with them exchanging pleasantries. 'Now then,' said Aidan handing them a couple of menus, 'what would you like?'

'This is very generous of you,' said Flats.

Sean was making friends with Jeeves who was loving the attention. He summoned a waiter; 'What would you two like to drink?'

'May I have an orange juice and lemonade please?' asked Andrea politely.

'Make mine a G and T please, with ice and a slice,' requested Flats.

'That will be two of those and a large whiskey for Aidan,' instructed Sean. The waiter nodded and left.

'So what can we do for you?' asked Aidan.

Flats handed him the file; 'These are pictures of some men we want to trace, especially the first two. They are responsible for the murder of two young police officers. I was hoping that you may know who they are.'

Aidan shook his head as he passed the pictures to Sean; 'What have you got yourself into? These are two of Frank Brennan's men, and they're a long way from home. The others work for Finnegan and Nolan; I've seen them at the abattoir but don't ask me for names.'

'I didn't realise just how deeply involved Seamus and Dara were with Brennan,' said Sean.

'It certainly explains a few things,' added Aidan, 'the two main thugs can normally be found hanging around with Brennan. He has a betting shop somewhere in Stoke which is his headquarters; we won't have anything to do with him.'

Sean passed the pictures back to Flats; 'This one is known as 'The Sleeve' because one of his arms is fully tattooed. The second one goes by the name of 'Slugs' because he is reputed to have killed several people. It's quite an apt name really, because he's a slimy character.'

'Well they are both wanted for murder and I will bring them to justice,' said Flats in a determined voice.

Andrea was looking very concerned and grabbed Flats' arm; 'This is getting too dangerous, I couldn't bear anything happening to you.'

'I don't intend to do anything stupid, but you have just

reminded me of something that I must do.'

The waiter came back with their drinks and took their food order. 'Changing the subject; how is Sir Basil now and what plans do you have for him?'

'We had a long conversation with Kenny and we've decided to enter him for the Grand National, he's a decent stayer and jumps very well,' said Sean.

'I have never had a bet on that race before, but I will now,' announced Andrea.

They enjoyed their meal and discussed many topics, including Frank Brennan and his suspected activities relating to race fixing and bribing jockeys.

'It's men like him who give the Irish a bad name; he's not popular with a lot of people back home in Ireland,' informed Aidan, 'if you need any additional help, unofficially of course, give us a call.'

'I'll bear that in mind,' replied Flats as he got up to leave, 'thank you for a lovely meal,' he said as he shook hands with his hosts.

Andrea also thanked them; 'That was smashing.'

As she drove them home Andrea could see that Flats was deep in thought. 'What's troubling you?'

'I was just thinking of those two unfortunate officers and their families. My hunch is that the two thugs known as The Sleeve and Slugs were present when poor Ben Collis was murdered. That reminds me; I have a report to write for the commissioner.'

When they got back to the cottage, Flats said that he was going to spend some time in the garden; Jeeves can let off a bit of steam.'

'I'll make you a cup of tea and bring it out to you.'

Andrea came out carrying two cups and after handing one to Flats, she sat by his side; 'Can I ask you a question?' He nodded. 'If those two brutes murdered Ben, why didn't they just shoot him too?'

'That's a good point; as Ben's killers tried to make it look like suicide, we could be looking for someone else. It was quite amateurish in its execution, if you forgive my choice of words. We need to see if Dicky has matched any prints to our current suspects.'

~~~~

The following morning when Flats and Andrea arrived at the police station, he went to see the Chief whilst she went to the incident room. The commissioner was with the Chief and another man in the office.

'Good morning Flats, this is Chief Superintendent Yeates, he wants an update on our suspects.'

'Of course; here is my report as you requested.'

'Thank you; but having read all the others, I am satisfied beyond all doubt that you cannot be held responsible for the deaths of the officers. There's no way it could have been foreseen or prevented. The most important job now is to apprehend the men responsible.'

'I had dinner with Kelly and Lynch last evening and they informed me, that the two men we want both work for Frank Brennan. Neither of them knows their real names, just the nicknames that they use. I've written them on the relevant pictures. What I did discover is that Brennan's base is at his Stoke premises, and it's believed his thugs are frequently there too.'

'That's good enough for me; I'll get a surveillance team on it right away. You can leave these two to me and my team,' said Yeates, 'I'll keep in touch.'

'Now then Flats,' started the commissioner, 'what do you intend to do with our three suspects?'

'First I want to double check with Dicky as to the finger prints he has lifted from the bottle and syringe. Then it's my intention to interrogate, and then charge, all of them for the murder of Ben Collis. I believe there was a fourth person present and I hope to get one of them to reveal who it was. If you'll excuse me gents, I'll get right on it.'

Dicky was waiting for him in the incident room; 'I have some good prints from the syringe and a couple from the bottle; excluding Finnegan's sister that is. None of them match Niall Finnegan's though. Andi and I are just about to take finger prints from both Nolan and Finnegan senior, so as soon as we're done we'll let you know our findings.'

Flats nodded just as WPC Knott called out to him. He crossed the room to her desk; 'I think we have a name for the gangster known as The Sleeve; he's Danny Mack of no fixed abode. If we're right, he did time some years ago for attempted robbery where some of those involved were tooled up. Give us a bit more time and we should be able to confirm it.'

Sergeant Hoskins asked if there was anything he could do; 'I'm fed up of twiddling my thumbs.'

'As a matter of fact there is; Dicky reckons that whoever wielded the syringe was left handed, can you get Niall to write something and let me know which hand he uses.'

'What about us?' asked Nick, 'what can Isla and I do?'

'Wait and be patient, until Dicky and Andi have taken the necessary finger prints, there's nothing for us to do. Although, thinking about it, we could discuss our strategy for dealing with them.'

The three of them sat around a desk chatting and making notes. Hoskins returned; 'He's right handed.'

Flats exhaled sharply; 'I expected as much; looking at our three suspects, I don't think either of them has the courage to kill someone. Something tells me that there was definitely a fourth individual involved and it is that person who did the necessary deed. We need to try and extract that information from the others and I have an idea that might just work. I think that we should have a cup of tea whilst we wait for Dicky to finish.'

Chapter Twenty Four

When Dicky and Andrea finally returned, they were smiling. 'I'll let my assistant fill you in.'

'The bottle was handled by Finnegan's sister, Nolan and one other person who we haven't identified yet. As for the syringe, there are only two different prints and one is

Seamus Finnegan. We think the other is this mysterious fourth person.'

'Can you let me have the bags containing both items, and the cigar butts? Nick; have Niall taken to an interview room, I want to start with him.'

A constable entered and informed them that Finnegan's lawyer had arrived and was demanding to talk to his client.

'Let him start with Niall but inform him that we will be interviewing him shortly. Well team, it looks like we will have to wait a little while longer to interrogate our suspects,' announced Flats.

Eventually the lawyer finished speaking with Niall and announced that he was ready for the interview to proceed.

Flats told Nick and Isla that they would have to take charge of proceedings. 'We have to do this by the book or there's no way we can get a conviction that would hold up in court.' Before they went to the room, Flats pulled Isla to one side, 'Here's what I want you to do,' he told her as he gave her a piece of paper. 'Do you think you can handle it?'

'I was trained by a master of interviewing techniques,

trust me, I got this, and I'm going to enjoy it.'

Inside the interview room, Nick and Isla sat opposite Niall and his lawyer while Flats took a seat away from them. After the usual introductions, the lawyer wanted to know why Flats was present.

'He is in overall charge of the investigation and as such, has every right to be here. Now let's get on,' said Nick.

'What is your connection to Frank Brennan?'

'I don't know anyone of that name.'

'That's interesting because previously you seemed to be perturbed when we suggested that we might inform him it was you who set him up.'

'My client has stated that he does not know anyone of that name,' interrupted the lawyer.

'Again, that's interesting, for your information we have several witnesses who will testify that the two of them were often seen at Kemble Farm together,' snapped Isla.

'Okay, so my client may know this person, that's not a crime, is it?'

'Frank Brennan is wanted in connection with the abduction of the horse known as Sir Basil and for race fixing offences,' said Nick. 'Your client's association with this man would suggest he may be involved, or at least know of his criminal activities.'

'That's a slanderous accusation Detective Inspector; I suggest you withdraw that statement.'

Isla then took over, 'Where were you on the day that Ben Collis was murdered?'

'I was at the abattoir with my father.'

'Are you quite sure? We do have evidence that you, and your father, were at Kemble Farm at the time.'

'You can't have.'

'In fact we have evidence that you were involved in the murder of Ben Collis.'

'That's rubbish, I wasn't there.'

Isla placed the syringe on the table; 'If you weren't there, HOW COME YOUR PRINTS ARE ON THIS?'

'THEY CAN'T BE, I was wearing gloves.'

The lawyer covered his eyes with his hand and shook his head.

'Niall Finnegan, I am charging you with the murder of

Mr. Ben Collis,' said Isla, 'take him back to his cell.'

Outside the room, Flats was the first to congratulate her; 'That was brilliant, now once the lawyer has spoken to Seamus Finnegan and Dara Nolan, we can have a go at them too.'

'I was shaking like a leaf in there but I think my adrenalin kicked in. Thank you Flats for giving me the confidence to tackle these interviews.'

'I'm impressed partner, remind to never piss you off,' said Nick.

'Okay you two, no rest for the wicked, let's prepare for the other interrogations,' ordered Flats.

The mood in the incident room was very cheerful as the rest of the team congratulated Isla and Nick.

Andrea was sitting with Dicky, who as usual, was sipping tea; 'Well done old boy, but you still don't know who actually injected the poor jockey.'

'One step at a time my friend, I will have his name before the day is out.'

An officer came in and told them that the lawyer had finished talking to Seamus Finnegan.

'Hoskins, would you be so kind as to have him taken to the interview room? And if you two are ready, shall we go?'

'Isla, do you mind if I take the lead this time? I don't think you should have all the fun,' asked Nick.

'Be my guest, I'll just hand you what you need.'

Once again the necessary introductions were made as Nick and Isla sat opposite Seamus Finnegan and his lawyer.

'Mr. Finnegan; can you explain why you removed your horse from the stable at Cheltenham racecourse?'

'It was nothing to do with me, my horse was stolen.'

'So how do you account for the fact that your son Niall was actively involved?'

The lawyer leant across and whispered something to his client.

'No comment,' was Finnegan's reply.

'Going back to my original question, why did you remove your horse?'

'I believe my client has answered that already.'

Isla placed a bag on the table. 'This is a cigar butt discarded by you at Kenny Race's stable. You will note the end is not cut evenly.'

Isla produced a second bag; 'This cigar butt was found near Sir Basil's stable at Cheltenham. The next one was found where the horse was transferred from a stolen horsebox into a horse trailer and finally; we have one found at Kemble Farm in the stable where Ben Collis was hanged.'

'All this is circumstantial, who's to say these butts are not different cigars discarded by different people?' insisted the lawyer.

'Look closely and you will see that all of them bear the same tear mark on their ends and we can firmly place you, Mr. Finnegan, at three of the locations I have mentioned. Now, although we are interested in the abduction of the horse, it's the murder of Ben Collis that concerns us the most.'

'My client denies all knowledge of the incident as he was elsewhere at the time.' Isla and Nick glanced at Flats briefly before Nick continued.

'Mr. Finnegan; why were you recently at Kemble Farm? Before you reply, I should make you aware that a team of officers were present on the same afternoon, myself included. We witnessed two of the men, who were with you; go to the place where the poor unfortunate officers were held and shot dead.'

The lawyer once again spoke quietly to Finnegan who grinned; 'What proof do you have of my client's involvement in the killing of the jockey?'

Isla produced two more bags. A puzzled look crossed Finnegan's face as he looked at the items. The colour drained from his face and he appeared concerned.

'These are what we believe you were looking for on that afternoon,' said Isla. Nick resumed; 'We witnessed you finding similar items that we had strategically placed at the farm. You obviously thought you had found the incriminating evidence, one of which you and your partner destroyed. Both the bottle and syringe have your finger prints on them. They have been verified as those used in the killing of Ben Collis. Mr. Finnegan, I am formally charging you with the murder of Mr. Ben Collis. Sergeant; have him taken back to his cell.'

'I didn't do it I tell you, I've been framed.' Turning to the lawyer, Nick asked if he would now like to speak to Dara Nolan.

'Yes, but I won't be very long,' he replied.

When the lawyer had left the room; Flats congratulated Nick and Isla. 'We now have two convictions but we still don't know who actually administered the injection.'

'Perhaps Nolan will shed some light,' suggested Isla.

'That interview needs to be handled slightly differently,' informed Flats, 'I would like to conduct this one; but first I want a word with Niall Finnegan.'

'Would you like me to have him brought here?'

'No thanks Nick; you and I are going to speak to him in his cell. I believe we can get him to spill the beans.'

The two men entered the cell; 'We've come to offer you a deal if you're interested,' said Flats. 'Your dad has just been charged with murder, the same as you.'

'You've got it all wrong; my dad had nothing to do with the murder, he wasn't there.'

'We have evidence placing your dad at the scene; what we really want to know is who injected Ben Collis.'

'I-I-I can't tell you,' replied Niall with a concerned look.

Flats nodded at Nick to leave. Outside the cell, he ushered him to a quiet corner; 'I have a very uneasy feeling about this, he seemed to be telling the truth.'

Chapter Twenty Five

Once the lawyer had finished speaking to Nolan in private, the two of them were ushered into the interview room. Nick made the necessary introductions after which Flats asked the lawyer if he would allow him to ask the questions. Following a quick exchange of glances with his client; he nodded in agreement.

'Thank you; Mr. Nolan, where were you on the day Ben Collis was murdered?'

'I was at the abattoir overseeing some deliveries.'

Flats produced the two evidence bags; 'Can you explain why your finger prints are on these? Before you answer, you should know that myself and members of my team were hiding at the farm when you found our strategically placed decoys. Only someone there at the time of the murder would have known about these, so we know that you were involved.'

After a brief conversation with his lawyer, he replied 'No comment.'

Flats whispered in Nick's ear; he nodded in response; 'Mr. Nolan, I am formally charging you with the murder of Mr. Ben Collis at Kemble Farm; officer, take him back to his cell.'

'You've got it all wrong; I didn't kill that jockey. I wasn't even there.'

'Would you like to tell us who did?' snapped Nick.

There was no reply from Nolan as he was led away. Isla could see from the look on Flats' face that he was concerned; 'I've seen that look before,' she said.

Without saying another word; Flats left the interview room and went to see the Chief. They talked for several minutes; 'I can't answer this one, as you well know, but I will speak to the commissioner.'

Flats returned to the incident room and sat down next to Andrea. Dicky could see something was troubling his friend; 'Would you like to talk about it?' he asked.

By now, Nick and Isla had joined them; 'We have three suspects, but only one has admitted that he was there when Ben was murdered. Both Finnegan and Nolan are denying that they were involved but their finger prints are on the syringe and bottle.'

Suddenly he stood up and went to the suspect's board. After several minutes he asked if someone would fetch him a flip chart and stand. When it arrived, he took a pen and began to draw. 'Excuse the crudity of the drawing; now we know how Ben was killed and we have established that Niall was present. Using the famous Sherlock Holmes analogy; and although it seems unlikely, if we assume that both Finnegan and Nolan are telling the truth, then we are looking for two or three other men. If they were both at the abattoir then the only explanation is that they gave the bottle and syringe to someone else. But why are Finnegan's prints on the syringe when they come in sealed bags?'

'Surely the answer is that he was involved,' said Nick.

'My dear fellow,' said Dicky, looking up from sipping his tea, 'sometimes we must look beyond the obvious. If Flats has doubts then there must be something amiss.'

'Do you think that Frank Brennan was involved? Suggested Andrea, 'after all, Aidan told us he was dangerous, and we know that Niall is friendly with, yet somewhat wary of him.'

'Of course; well done Andi, he's the one who had most to lose if Ben's accusations were made public, that's assuming our information is correct regarding his involvement with race fixing.'

'I still don't get it; we have enough evidence to convict Finnegan and Nolan and yet we're looking for two or three others,' argued Nick.

'It's a question of logic,' answered Flats, 'we have two men protesting their innocence even though they've seen our evidence. Guilty men would normally go quietly and accept the situation. We need to have a chat with Niall and lean on him a little; he may just crumble and give us what we need. Isla, would you come with me, it's time for you to play the good cop.'

On the way to the cells, Flats explained how he wanted to proceed. They entered the cell and sat opposite Niall; 'What do you want now?' he demanded.

'Do you realise the trouble you are in?' questioned Flats. 'Your father and his partner Dara Nolan are denying that they were present at the killing of Ben Collis. The commissioner wants to close the case which will mean that you will take the full blame. How long do you think he will get DS White?'

'Twenty five years, possibly thirty I should think,' she answered, 'his dad will do at least fifteen for aiding and abetting.'

'Is there anything else that you would like to tell us?' enquired Flats.

'I can't, he'd kill me.'

'I assume you are referring to Frank Brennan.'

'We know he was there,' informed Isla, 'Dara let it slip during his interview.'

'He's not a man you cross; I wish I'd never met him, I never wanted to hurt that jockey.'

'Was he the one who used the syringe?' probed Flats.

Niall shook his head, 'Frank would never get his hands dirty, he orders someone else to do that.'

Flats stood up, 'We'll be back shortly, in the meantime, can we get you anything?'

'A decent cup of coffee and a pack of cigarettes wouldn't go amiss.'

'Isla, would you see to that? I need to speak to the chief.'

Flats entered the chief's office; 'Any luck Larry?'

'Yes indeed; the commissioner has agreed, but only if we get a statement that leads to a conviction.'

'Okay, leave it with me; I believe we may just have it before the end of the day.' Flats left the office and asked Isla to join him. After briefing her, they returned to Niall's cell.

'I have some good news for you, it has been agreed that you will receive a much shorter sentence in exchange for a full statement that includes the names of the others who were present on that fateful day. We already know about you and Frank; so who else was there?'

Before Niall could answer, Nick came rushing into the cell and informed Flats that he was wanted in the chief's office immediately.

'We'll continue this chat later,' he told Niall before leaving with Isla.

'You wanted me?' asked Flats as he entered the chief's office.

'Yes; I've just received word from CS Yeates; they tried to arrest Frank Brennan and his henchmen in Stoke. Apparently it quickly turned ugly and there was a fire fight resulting in a few deaths, one of which was Frank Brennan. He tried to shoot his way out as he attempted to get to his car. Yeates is coming here tomorrow and has requested that you are present; he will give us a full brief then. His team have requested a search warrant for the betting shop, hopefully that will reveal more of his illegal activities.'

Flats frowned; 'That's a tad disappointing, I was looking forward to interrogating Frank Brennan. The world will be a little safer without him though; do we know if either of the pc's killers have been apprehended?'

The chief shook his head; 'He never said, the only one he mentioned personally was Brennan.'

'Thanks for the update, I should get back to Niall Finnegan, he may feel more like talking when he hears the news of Frank Brennan.'

Flats went to the incident room and asked his team to gather round. He then informed them of what the chief had told him. 'We will know much more tomorrow, now I must finish my discussion with Niall; Isla, bring a notepad, I think we will need one.'

They entered the cell and once seated, Flats gave Niall the news. The young man looked very relieved for a moment; 'What about his men?'

'We won't know the full story until the morning, now would you like to tell us who killed Ben Collis?'

'I need to know who else has been arrested and on what charges before I'll tell you everything, but I will admit that Frank Brennan was there.'

'Okay, we'll leave it at that for now. The offer of a reduced sentence in exchange for what you know, still stands, you have my word.'

Outside the cell, Isla held up the notepad; 'I still have plenty of empty pages left.'

Flats smiled; 'I'm sure we'll fill up many pages tomorrow, now let's get back to the team.'

He crossed the room to where Andrea was sitting with Jeeves; 'Here's a tenner, go and buy some treats for everybody, they deserve it, after that we can go home.'

Chapter Twenty Six

The next morning at breakfast, Isla was keen to know what Flats was planning for the day ahead. 'Everything depends on what chief superintendent Yeates tells us.'

'Will you release Finnegan and Nolan?'

'No chance, those two are involved in some way with race fixing, and there is definitely a link between them and Frank Brennan.'

'Well I'm not sorry that he's dead,' said Andrea, 'he was dangerous.'

'You should never speak ill of the dead, no matter what a person may have done,' said Flats. 'Anyway; when someone like that dies you can guarantee there's another person waiting to fill his shoes.'

After breakfast they made their way to the station. Dicky was waiting for Andrea; 'Come with me my dear, we have work to do, more finger print checking I'm afraid.'

Flats went to the chief's office which was a little overcrowded. 'You know everyone here except D.I. Spencer; he's the chief superintendent's right hand man. I asked Crookes and White to join us as this concerns them as well.'

DS Yeates began his brief; 'As you've heard, Frank Brennan is dead. We tried to arrest him and the others at his shop but they produced weapons. He was shot when he opened fire at one of my officers who was seriously wounded, but we are hopeful that he will make a full recovery. Two more of his men were killed in the ensuing gun fight, one of which was the man known as 'Slug'. You may be interested in another couple who we arrested; Rory Whelan and Patrick O'Donnell, they've been taken to Bath police station for questioning. The chief informed me that you are investigating race fixing and fraud, so we have boxed up everything from the betting shop.'

'If you'd like to tell me where you want it, I'll get the boys to unload the van,' offered D.I. Spencer.

Flats turned to Isla; 'Would you show the D.I. to our incident room, I think we should put it in one corner of that room.'

'I can spare you one more member of staff if you require it,' offered the chief.

'I'll see what WPC Knott thinks and let you know; now if you'll excuse me gentlemen, I need to speak to Niall Finnegan now I have the facts about Brennan.'

He entered the incident room and went to WPC Knott's desk; 'There's more work for you if you don't mind. The chief says you can have one more person to help if you need it. See if you can find anything relating to race fixing. Isla; are you ready to resume our chat with Niall?'

'Yes, notepad ready and pen poised.'

Once inside the cell, Niall was anxious to know who had been arrested; 'Tell me what happened, I need to know.'

'There was a shoot out at Frank Brennan's betting shop; apart from him, the man you knew as Slug and one other were all shot dead. Several arrests were made including Rory Whelan and Patrick O'Donnell. Now will you tell us who else was present when Ben Collis was murdered?'

'I want to make it clear that I didn't want any part in it, I've been having nightmares every night since that day. The trouble is that you never said no to Frank if you valued your life. Rory and Patrick were both there too, along with the big boss.'

'Who is this big boss and where does he come from?' asked Flats.

'I really don't know; I've only seen him a couple of times and he never spoke directly to me.'

'Could you describe him to a police artist so we have an idea of what he looks like?' urged Flats.

Niall nodded; 'You have to catch him before you release me or I'm a dead man.'

'Relax, we have several men in custody; any one of them could be accused of having supplied the information. I'll requisition a police artist and you can give him the description. We will also need you to give us a written statement.'

'I understand ….. But there is one more person involved who I really don't wish to name.'

'You will have to give us all names if you wish the court to grant you a shorter sentence,' Flats reminded him. As he stood up he turned to Nick; 'Have Niall taken to an interview room so that he can make his statement. Make sure he has something to drink and anything else, within reason.'

'Leave it to me; I'll stay with him,' replied Nick.

Flats went to the chief's office and gave him the news.

'I will ring and inform the Chief Superintendent to be ready with his men. If there's someone above Brennan then he will be highly dangerous.'

'If we can bust this ring then Niall will deserve a lighter sentence, and that's something I never thought I would admit to,' said Flats, 'in the meantime I will go and see how the team is getting on.'

Andrea and Dicky were waiting for him; 'The additional prints did belong to Frank Brennan,' said Dicky.

'Niall confirmed that he was there that day along with someone else who he claims is the big boss. Don't ask me who he is because Niall doesn't know his name. We should have a sketch of him later.' He crossed the room to WPC Knott's desk; 'So how are you getting on?'

'Very well actually; there's some interesting stuff

amongst all the paperwork you gave us. We are compiling a list of those involved with race fixing and some who we think may have been subject to a protection racket, thankfully Frank kept some helpful records. It will probably take us another day before we are ready to confirm names for you; I think we will need some bigger cells.'

Flats called to Isla; 'Have Seamus Finnegan taken to an interview room, I think that he might be ready to talk.'

Once they were in the room, Seamus asked for his lawyer to be present; 'You won't need him today,' answered Flats. 'Firstly you should be aware that Frank Brennan is dead and your son has confirmed, in a written statement, that you were not present at the hanging, however, we do have evidence of race fixing in which you are implicated. We are in the process of rounding up all the others involved. This is your chance to come clean and tell us about your involvement and all that you know, it's up to you.'

'I didn't do that much ….. But I was forced into taking Sir Basil out of Cheltenham because of death threats against my family. I admit that we got a little greedy and saw the race fixing as a chance to earn a little extra. The business has been struggling and I've become accustomed to a certain standard of life.'

'Okay, putting that aside for the moment there is the matter of the firearm that you threatened the police with. Why would you need such a weapon?'

'It was for my own protection; Frank Brennan is not a man you can trust; and as for his boss.'

'Who is this boss? Do you know his name?' urged Flats.

Seamus shook his head; 'No I don't; I only ever saw him once, but rumour has it he's worse than Frank Brennan, I just wish that I'd never got involved.'

'Well you're going to pay for it now,' said Isla, 'you're facing a few years inside.'

'If you give us a fully detailed and signed statement, we'll try and arrange for you to be sent to a different prison away from the others,' offered Flats. 'I'll have someone come and take your statement and get you a hot drink.'

Outside the room, Flats asked Isla if she would like to conduct the same interview with Dara Nolan.

'Yes please; I notice you have gone soft with Seamus, I never thought that I would see that.'

'We have him banged to rights, a little humility now and we should get all the information needed to wrap up the murder and the betting scandal.' He took something from his jacket pocket; 'Give this to Seamus, I'll never smoke it and I know he'll enjoy it.'

Back in the incident room, Andrea was waiting with a drawing; 'This is based on the description that Niall Finnegan gave.'

Flats took the piece of paper from her and looked at the image; 'I don't believe it, is he serious?'

'That was my thought too.'

'I need to speak to Larry, immediately.'

Chapter Twenty Seven

The chief inspector was rifling through some papers when Flats entered the office. He handed him the picture; 'This is a sketch of the top man in all of this; can you get in touch with CS Yeates, and ask him to meet me here as soon as possible?'

'Yeates and his men are currently rounding up a list of

suspects; do we have any idea who this person is?'

'Yes we do, not only do we have a name but we also have a location, here, see for yourself. You must get hold of the Chief Superintendent immediately and tell him that we know who the top boss is. I'll be in the incident room waiting for his response.'

Andrea was looking very pleased with herself. 'I can see you're dying to tell me something,' said Flats.

'The Sarge and I have been looking through the footage from the Cheltenham meeting, come and see what we've found.'

Flats looked at the frozen picture on the screen; 'Well who'd have believed that?'

'There's more, Lynne has begun some background checks and found a connection between them.'

Dicky had joined them; 'My guess old chap is that we have just found the owner of the missing finger prints from the syringe.'

Flats turned to see his friend holding up a crisp one pound note. He thought for a moment and then nodded.

'You two are incorrigible,' said Andrea with a smile.

The Chief entered the room; 'I have spoken to Chief Superintendent Yeates and he is on his way here right now with an armed unit. His eta is ….. Forty minutes from now,' said the Chief as he checked his watch.

'We have time for another cup of tea then,' said Dicky.

'And, it will give me time to take Jeeves for a walk,' said Flats.

'I'll come with you,' insisted Andrea. As they walked, she asked Flats if he believed that Niall was right with his accusation.

'Why would he lie? There is a possibility that he's putting two and two together and making five. Just because someone is present it doesn't mean they are the big boss. Either way, we'll know for sure when he's brought in for questioning; especially if the finger prints are his.'

When they returned from their walk, CS Yeates was waiting in the Chief's office studying the artist sketch.

'I understand from the Chief Inspector that you know this man; what's he like?'

'He has always been a perfect gentleman as far as I'm concerned. I certainly would not have believed that he's a top criminal boss.'

'Can I assume that you know where we can find him?'

Flats nodded; 'Yes and it's not far from here.'

'Right then, we'd better go and pick him up.'

They drove the relatively short distance to the warehouse; where, on arrival, Flats was surprised at how far the builders had got with the security building. As they approached the offices, there was an ambulance parked outside.

'Let me go in first,' suggested Flats, 'he won't suspect anything. You and one of your men should come with me as it would look like you could be contractors.'

The Chief Superintendent paused for a moment and then nodded his agreement; 'If anything goes wrong, you get out of the building immediately and let me and my team take over.' He signalled for two of his team to take up positions by the entrance to the warehouse and then followed Flats into the offices. As they climbed the stairs, the ambulance men came down.

'Sorry gents,' said one of them, 'you can't go any further, we believe this might be a crime scene and we are waiting for the police to arrive.'

Yeates flashed his badge; 'We are the police.' He told Flats to wait with the member of his team and went outside. They could hear him giving orders to his men to secure the area and then he called for backup.

Turning to the ambulance men he asked them what had happened.

'We answered an emergency call saying that a man was taken ill and struggling for breath. When we got here we found Mr. Silva slumped over at his desk, he was already dead. The secretary is, understandably, very hysterical.'

Flats heard the conversation and suggested that he should go first as he was known to her. When he got to the offices he found Stirling's Secretary sobbing uncontrollably. As soon as she saw him, she flung her arms around him looking for some comfort. Eventually Julie had calmed down enough to explain that they had several clients visit during the day, looking to make use of the warehouse.

'Do you have the name of the visitors?' asked Flats.

'Yes, I have a list here. The last of them was a couple and they came out looking distressed and said that Mr. Silva had just slumped over his desk. That's when I called for an ambulance. I tried to revive him but he was unresponsive.'

'Was he still breathing when you found him?'

'Y-y-yes, I think so.'

Flats made for the telephone in the room and dialled; 'Put me through to the Chief Inspector please, quickly ….. Hello Larry, can you tell Andrea and Dicky that I need them both at Stirling Silva's warehouse immediately, unfortunately the man is dead, I'll explain more later.'

When he was certain that Julie had calmed down, Flats went into Stirling's office where Yeates was waiting. 'There's something not quite right; if he is the big boss, where are all of his men? My team tells me that apart from a couple of forklift driver's there's only construction and building staff on site.'

Flats acknowledged him as he studied the body. He walked around the desk looking from all angles.

'What are you thinking?' asked Yeates.

Flats looked at him with a frown; 'There are no obvious signs that he was killed, I can't see any marks to suggest that; but his cup is on its side and someone has cleaned up most of the spillage. He wasn't that old and he seemed perfectly healthy when I last saw him so could he have been poisoned?'

Moving close to the Chief Superintendent he whispered;

'When the uniformed officers arrive,' he nodded towards Julie, 'I want her taken in to give a statement and I want a description of the last two clients. This is a list of visitors in order of arrival. Can you get one of your men to stand guard in this room whilst we take a look around the rest of the site?'

When they were out of the offices, Yeates asked Flats if he thought that Stirling Silva could have been murdered.

'We have to consider it; especially if he's supposed to be the big boss. I have a top pathologist on his way and he will shed some light on anything suspicious. Now, would you mind getting your men to clear the site?'

'No problem; I'll also make a call to customs and have this site closed. I bet those guys will be interested in some of the items in the warehouse.'

It wasn't long before the sound of police sirens filled the air and several cars pulled into the site. Flats was pleased to see Nick and Isla amongst the officers. He informed them that Julie was to be taken to the station for questioning and to make her statement.

'We need her to give us descriptions of the last two clients; a man and a woman. Something doesn't feel right.'

'That old gut feeling again,' said Isla.

'Precisely; who would kill the top man? And why?'

'What would you like us to do?' asked Nick.

'CS Yeates has had his men clear all personnel from the site, so can you secure the place and have several officers guarding the site until we've finished this investigation? You may find that customs will take over when they arrive.'

Dicky arrived with Andrea. Flats briefed him on what was needed.

'We will get to work and let you know our findings in due course. Where will you be?'

'I'm going nowhere until you've done your initial investigation.'

'Okay Andi, let us see what we can uncover.'

Chapter Twenty Eight

Around half an hour later, Dicky and Andrea emerged from the office building.

'What do we know Dicky?' asked Flats.

'When we lifted the body from the desk, there was a small blood stain just below the collar. This indicates, I believe, that Stirling was stabbed with a Hypodermic needle, and my guess is that it was the same type used in the murder of Ben Collis. The side of the neck and the angle suggests a left-handed person. I will have to do the autopsy before confirming the exact cause of death.'

'That means that Stirling could not have killed Ben because he was right handed,' added Andrea.

'So Niall Finnegan has been lying to us; there was someone else at the stables that day. Good work you two, I need to get back to the station.'

'I can give you a lift on our way to the morgue,' offered Dicky, 'you can have Jeeves back too.'

Back at the station, Flats went to see the Chief and explained the situation at the warehouse. 'As soon as Isla or Nick returns I'll question Niall Finnegan further, the deal we offered is now off the table.'

'I can sit in with you; if you like,' offered the Chief.

'That would be good; I'm in the right frame of mind to tackle him right now.'

The Chief left his office briefly and when he returned he informed Flats that Sergeant Hoskins would have Niall Finnegan taken to an interview room.

Several minutes later the Sergeant knocked on the Chief's door; 'Ready when you are sir, room two.'

The two men proceeded to the room where Niall was seated. Flats wasted no time; 'Who else was there when Ben Collis was murdered?'

'I told you everything; honest.'

'Really? Every one you named is right-handed. We happen to know that whoever stabbed Ben with the syringe was left-handed, so I ask you again, who else was present?'

'I-I-I told you already.'

'Well I don't believe you; the deal is off, Sergeant, have him taken back to his cell.'

Once Niall was removed, the Chief turned to Flats;

'Where does that leave us now?'

'He's hiding something; let's see what Dicky and Andrea come up with. I think I'll drive over to the morgue and check on their progress.'

Dicky was pleased to see him when he arrived; 'Stirling was indeed stabbed in the same manner as Ben Collis. My guess is that the same person was responsible in both incidents. He was injected with the same substance as Ben Collis, the amount used would have knocked him out almost immediately, but that didn't kill him; he was suffocated. Whoever did this probably had some military training; as there are no fibres around the face I assume they just used their hands.'

'So you think we are looking for an ex-soldier or possibly someone similarly trained.'

'That would be my guess Flats ….. Fancy a pint later?'

'I think we all deserve one; now hopefully Miss Noted will have given us decent descriptions of the couple who visited Sterling; I'll see you later.'

'If it's okay with Dicky, I'll come with you,' said Andrea.

'Of course dear girl, I can finish up here.'

Back at the station Isla was waiting with a couple of drawings of the latest suspects. Flats looked at the faces and shook his head; 'Really? Now things are beginning to make sense.'

Andrea took a look at them and then handed them back; 'I'll speak to Lynne,' and she hurried away.

Flats decided to follow her. After a brief conversation between the two women, Lynne reached for her phone.

'You're right; she was released two days ago,' said Lynne as she put the phone down.

Andrea turned to Flats, 'As you know, the woman in that picture is Deidre Finnegan and she IS left handed. Whoever the man is; he has to be connected to her.'

'Now it makes sense as to why Niall didn't want to tell us who else was involved in the murder of Ben Collis. Hoskins, would you come with me please?'

The two men strode purposefully to the cell where Niall Finnegan was being held. 'We now know that your aunt stabbed Ben Collis with the syringe; now tell me who this is,' demanded Flats holding up the picture.

'Th-that's her boyfriend; Ali Kantay ….. And he's a very nasty piece of work.'

'Was he there with your aunt when Ben was killed?'

'N-no, I've told you everything now,' replied Niall.

Flats left the cells and headed to the Chief's office; 'We know who the killers are; this is a job for CS Yeates and his men. If we can locate Deidre Finnegan then I think we will find her boyfriend; one, 'Ali Kantay'. One of them murdered Sterling Silva and, I believe, Ben Collis.'

'That's great work, leave it with me and I'll take care of things from here.'

Flats returned to the incident room and informed every one of the latest developments. 'Thank you all for your excellent work.'

'Hang on a minute,' cried Andrea, 'we still don't know who the last set of finger prints on the syringe belong to. And I'm puzzled; why was Sterling murdered?'

'I can't answer your second question but I am certain the finger prints belong to either Deidre Finnegan or Ali Kantay. When we have them in custody, you can help check their prints to confirm it. Right now we should check with the forensics team to see if they uncovered anything from Sterling's office.'

He turned to Isla; 'Do you know if forensics are still at the warehouse?'

'They have dropped off several items and some boxes containing files and paperwork found in the offices. Nick and I are going to assist with sifting through it all.'

'Very good; do we have Julie Noted's statement?'

'I believe Nick has it; talk of the devil.'

'I assume that remark was aimed at me,' said Nick with a smile.

'Yes it was; I was asking for Julie's statement,' answered Flats.

Nick handed him a thin folder and after thanking him, Flats sat down to peruse it. After several minutes, he closed the folder and sat staring into the air. Andrea sat down next to him; 'You look deep in thought, is everything alright?'

'To be honest with you; I don't know, my gut is telling me that something doesn't quite fit, I'm going to call it a day and come at it fresh in the morning.'

~~~~

After a restless night, Flats was up early and was sat at

the kitchen table rifling through the paperwork pertaining to the case when Andrea came into the room. 'Would you like another cup of tea?' she asked.

Flats nodded, 'Yes please, and while you're at it, do you fancy frying a bit of bacon?'

'Anything else with it, sir?'

'Now you mention it; A sausage or two, an egg, and a few beans would go down a treat, thank you.'

'In other words, cheeky, you'd like a full English. Have you found something else?' she enquired.

'I'm not sure, everything now points to Deidre Finnegan and her boyfriend, called Ali Kantay, but something still doesn't sit right with me. Hopefully, it will come to me later at the station. Right now I need to check to see if we have any fresh eggs for my breakfast, come on Jeeves.'

A few minutes later, he returned clutching three eggs, 'One each,' he declared handing them to Andrea.

Isla came into the kitchen, yawning.

'Still tired?' asked Flats.

'It was a late night, Knotty and me got hung up on

checking all the paperwork from Silva's office.'

'Was there anything of interest?'

'There was one thing we found that's puzzling, a plane ticket to Mexico. We weren't sure if it was significant so we put it to one side for you.'

'Well done, if you're ready Andi, let's go.'

When they entered the incident room, WPC Knott was already there working away.

'Don't you ever stop?' asked Flats jokingly.

'I can't help it, something was niggling away in my brain and I wanted to check it out. Did Isla tell you about the plane ticket?'

'Yes she did, can I see it?'

Flats looked at it, and then studied the board.

Nick entered, 'Flats, the chief would like a word.'

He handed the ticket back to Lynne and went to the chief's office. 'You wanted to see me?'

'Yes, bad news I'm sorry to say. Yeates and his men have been looking for Deidre Finnegan and her boyfriend. They're both in Ireland and have been for a day or so.'

Flats nodded and returned to the incident room. He stared intently at the board, his eyes flickering at the photos and notes. His attention was broken by a shout from Lynne.

'We've got something!'

He walked over to her desk and she handed him a piece of paper, 'That links Deidre Finnegan to the bet fixing.'

'That's good work; where's that plane ticket?'

She handed him the slip of paper. After a quick glance he placed it back in front of her and pointed at it. Lynne frowned, and then with a raised eyebrow, looked at Flats.

'Okay, I'm on it. Give me a bit of time and I'll get back to you.'

Andi was puzzled, 'What are you thinking?'

'Can you do me a favour? Call Dicky and ask him to meet us here as soon as he can. Tell him, now would be most convenient.'

Flats left the room and went to find Nick. 'I have a job for you, can you fetch Julie Noted? I need to ask her some more questions.'

'What if she refuses to come?'

Flats shot him a firm glance; 'It's not a request.'

'I understand, I'll grab one of the lads and go myself.'

Dicky arrived and was curious as to why he had been summoned. 'What's the urgency Flats old boy?'

'I believe I will need your services, urgently. Let's get a cup of tea and I'll explain.'

Andrea joined them; 'Will you please tell me what's going through your mind pops,' she demanded.

'My dear girl, have you not noticed how we've been chasing shadows. Miss Noted gave us descriptions of the last two people who entered Sterling's office and we connected them to Deidre Finnegan and her man friend. If our intelligence is correct, it couldn't have been them because they are in Ireland. Either we are wrong with our assumption, or, as I suspect, she's lied to us and I want to know why.'

As they were drinking tea and waiting, an excited WPC Knott scurried towards them; 'You are not going to believe this,' she gabbled in her enthusiasm as she handed Flats a piece of paper.

After reading it, Flats sighed heavily before slumping

back in his chair deep in thought. He moved his hand to his lips with his index finger pointing upwards. Then he seemed to wave his finger slightly from side to side before touching it back to his lips. Several times he repeated this coupled with some slight head movements. Suddenly he spoke; 'Well done Lynne, I need to see the file on the bet fixing.'

Andrea was about to scream in frustration when Flats handed her the piece of paper. She looked at it and then showed Dicky before the two of them went to the incident room where Flats and Lynne were flicking through some papers.

Chapter Twenty Nine

It was later that day that Nick returned to the station with Julie Noted. Flats asked him to take her to an interview room and make her comfortable. He then spoke to Hoskins who followed Nick to the room.

'Isla, I would like you to conduct this interview; you'll need these papers and this ……. Oh and not forgetting these,' he said handing her several sheets of paper. 'Dicky and I will be observing from the next room; just remember that this is an informal chat to confirm what she has already told us.' Nick returned and Flats told him to liaise with Isla and that the two of them will be speaking to Julie. Larry joined Flats and Dicky in the side room as the discussion began.

'I am intrigued Flats, why are we in here?'

'To observe, she's hiding something,' replied Flats.

Isla began; 'Thank you Miss Noted for agreeing to talk to us again, I want to begin by clarifying your statement. We are desperate to catch Mr. Silva's killer and wondered if there was something else you might have remembered. Please, read this again and then confirm if it is accurate or you would like to add something to it.' She handed over a sheet of paper.

Julie could be seen reading it, and after a couple of minutes, 'Yes, that's true, there's nothing else to add.'

'Thank you, would you mind signing it a second time and put today's date after your signature?'

Before she had finished writing her name, Flats burst into the room. Isla immediately changed her intonation and demeanor. 'Julie Noted, I am arresting you for the murder of Mr. Stirling Silva.' Nick, with help from Hoskins, handcuffed her as Isla read out her rights.

Flats turned to Dicky; 'Now it's over to you and your assistant,' he said with a smile.

'I'll get my bag and collect her at the same time.'

Larry and Flats returned to the incident room where Lynne was still hard at work with her team. 'We should have the financial records soon to see if we can uncover more proof of her involvement in the betting scandal.'

'What made you suspect her? Are you sure she was involved?' urged Larry.

'We've been missing one suspect to match up a set of fingerprints. We also know that Sterling's killer, and Ben's, was left handed. As soon as Julie Noted began to sign her name, it gave me confirmation of my memory that she too is left-handed. The final piece was uncovered by WPC Knott. We all assumed she was Miss Julie Noted, but she was, in fact, Mrs. Noted. Apparently her husband was an accountant who died in suspicious circumstances about eighteen months ago. Her maiden name was Brennan and Frank Brennan is her older brother, and the more we dug the more we uncovered. Like her brother, she's a wrong 'un and according to our information, ex-military. We think poor Sterling was innocent and paid the price for her to escape. The plane ticket was in her name, she was planning to flee the country. What got me thinking was that every time I met with Sterling, he was always alone, if he was a big boss, he would certainly have a couple of heavies with him at all times.'

'That's great work, but why give false information about the last people to see Sterling?'

'My guess is that she intended to throw us off the scent long enough for her to make her getaway. All we need now is for Dicky to match up the fingerprints and my work is done.'

There was an anxious wait until Andrea entered the room with a beaming smile. 'You were right once again pops, perfect match.'

Flats turned to the chief; 'I guess that's me done, I'll let your team finish up from here.'

When everyone was assembled in the incident room, Flats thanked them for their hard work and suggested they should all meet later for a few celebratory drinks. 'Come on Andi, let's go home.' Jeeves sprang to his feet and followed the two of them out of the station.

Later that evening as Flats was getting ready to go out,

Isla came home. 'I thought that you might like to know that Deidre Finnegan has been taken into custody.'

'What about her friend Kantay?' he asked.

'You'll never believe it, but he's an undercover cop and apparently, glad to finish that assignment.'

'That would make sense,' said Flats nodding.

As they were driving to the pub, Flats looked at Andi; 'You know, I've been thinking, we deserve a holiday.'

'That sounds like a brilliant idea,' she answered.

The End

Other books in this series :-

A Lady Came Knocking

The Missing Prey

All Bets Are Off

~~~~~~

Look out for the next adventure

Make Mine a Double

Printed in Great Britain
by Amazon

78064652R00133